I'm
我 識出版社
17buy.com.tw

I'm

我識出版社
17buy.com.tw

I'm

我識出版社
17buy.com.tw

I'm

我識出版社
17buy.com.tw

6到60歲都學得會的
超簡單
英語會話

使用說明

Point 1

拋磚引玉的章節介紹

每一個章節會在開端點出該篇章的主題介紹，讀者可以細讀每一章的主題簡介，先瞭解不同章節的學習主題及內容，可以輕鬆掌握並融入各個主題的英語會話學習。

打招呼時需要的句子

　　試著想想看，如果我們遇到認識的人，用我們自己的語言通常必須先說什麼？在對話中又會提到哪些事情呢？

　　應該都會是先從「你好！」開始吧？接著可能會說「最近好嗎？」、「過得怎麼樣呢？」，並且表現出很高興見到對方的樣子。當談話進行一陣子之後，或許必須先告辭，在離開之前免不了要加上幾句禮貌性的話語，表達希望能再次見面、祝福或任何好聽的用語。

　　先讓我們來看看，這些情境在英語中要如何表達。

Point 2

不可忽略的發音語調

學習章節中的主要內容及實用對話，皆標示出重要的連音及抑揚頓挫的語調，學習運用標準的發音和語調，不必擔心與老外雞同鴨講，因為老外一定聽得懂。

Point 3

彙整筆記掌握學習精髓

針對各個不同的學習主題內容，貼心的為讀者彙整相關的句型筆記及小叮嚀（Tips），讓讀者在學習的過程中，能精確掌握每一個章節所學習的內容與精髓。

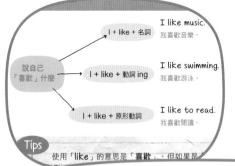

Tips

　　使用「like」的意思是「喜歡」，但如果是「非常喜歡」的情況，我們可以用「love」，例如：「I love reading.」、「I love to swim.」　或「Do you love playing football?」……等用法。

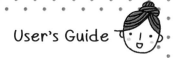

Point 4

淺顯易懂的實用對話

每一章節利用相關的教學內容，精選出 2 至 3 組的生活實用相關對話，跟老外溝通不必再比手畫腳，套用簡單的會話句型，輕鬆照樣造句開口說。

Hello, Will.
How's it going?
你好，威廉。
你好嗎？

So-so, thanks.
And you?
普普通通，謝謝。妳呢？

Good. Glad to meet you.
很好，很高興見到你。

Glad to meet you,
too. What's up?
我也很高興見到妳。
最近過得怎麼樣呢？

Nothing special.
What about you?
別的。你呢？

Fine. I'm doing w
actually.
很好，我

Point 5

附贈琅琅上口的MP3

特別邀請專業中外籍教師錄製每一章節的精選實用對話，標準的發音及語調，即使書本不在身邊，也能隨時練習聽力，讓你邊走邊聽。

★ 本書附贈 CD 片內容音檔為 MP3 格式 ★

(MP3) 18-03

生活會話「超簡單」 (MP3) 18-03

凱特・史密斯（Kate Smith）肚子
Smith）建議她去看醫生……

作者序 Preface

　　想要認真學英文的人，大概都曾在心裡有過這個疑問：到底怎麼樣才能把英文說好？要怎麼學習才能加強英文能力？語言是需要練習才能熟練的技能，語言技能的基礎是聽、說、讀及寫，必須時常練習聽力，累積大量的閱讀，並且勇敢開口說，逐步建構足以理解語言的骨架。並進一步將過程中學習的單字和片語，使用在不同的書寫體例中以學習正確和適宜的寫法。

　　聽力似乎很簡單，但許多人可能在心裡都很困惑，為什麼怎麼練習都還是聽不懂？不能理解外國人在說什麼，要練習口說也說不好，常常在情境中卻不知道該如何使用英語，學過的東西甚至沒辦法正確地發音，有的時候外國人還聽不懂自己在講什麼。因為不只是知道單字、片語，聽懂、讀懂和說得出正確的句子而已，正確的發音方式也是促進聽力和口說能力的重要因素。

　　因此，我們特別推出這本包含各種日常生活情境的英語會話書，囊括在日常生活中真實發生的狀況，除了可以學習到日常生活中的英語會話，讀者將可以學習發音（pronunciation）、句子中的抑揚頓挫（intonation）及連音（linking）的技巧，讓讀者可以說得更加自然。《圖解 6 到 60 歲都學得會的超簡單英語會話》搭配美國母語使用者（American native speaker）的發音教學，透過各種形式的句子，包括普遍的正式用法或非正式的用法，讓讀者瞭解與不同的對象交談時如何應對較為恰當。

　　最後，希望讀者在閱畢《圖解 6 到 60 歲都學得會的超簡單英語會話》和聆聽隨書附贈的 MP3 後，可以更加熟悉英語的發音並有益於增進口說的能力，那將是對我和編輯群最大的鼓舞與獎勵。

Thipthida Butchui
2014.02

目錄

Contents

目錄　Contents

PART 1

Chapter 1

第一章
最近好嗎？
Greetings

打招呼時需要的句子

試著想想看，如果我們遇到認識的人，用我們自己的語言通常必須先說什麼？在對話中，又會提到哪些事情呢？

應該都會是先從「你好！」開始吧？接著可能會說「最近好嗎？」、「過得怎麼樣呢？」，並且表現出很高興見到對方的樣子。當談話進行一陣子之後，或許必須先告辭，在離開之前免不了要加上幾句禮貌性的話語，表達希望能再次見面、祝福或任何好聽的用語。

先讓我們來看看，這些情境在英語中要如何表達。

正式的招呼語（Formal Greeting）

　　「正式的招呼語」即我們遇見已經認識，但不太熟識的人時，或者是第一次與某人見面時所用的開場白，我們應該要怎麼樣說會比較適當呢？

表達「**你好！**」可以這麼說：

Good morning!
早安！

Good afternoon.
午安。

Hello!
你好！
（任何時間都可用）

你好！

Good evening.
晚上好。

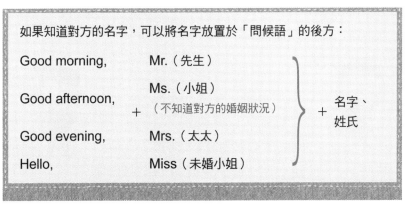

如果知道對方的名字，可以將名字放置於「問候語」的後方：

Good morning,	Mr.（先生）	
Good afternoon,	+ Ms.（小姐） （不知道對方的婚姻狀況）	+ 名字、姓氏
Good evening,	Mrs.（太太）	
Hello,	Miss（未婚小姐）	

Good morning,
Mr. Smith.
早安，史密斯先生。

Good afternoon,
Ms. Srinam.
午安，絲莉南小姐。

Good evening,
Mrs. Smith.
晚上好，史密斯太太。

Hello, Mr. Morgan.
你好，摩根先生。

詢問「**你好嗎？過得怎麼樣呢？**」可以這麼說：

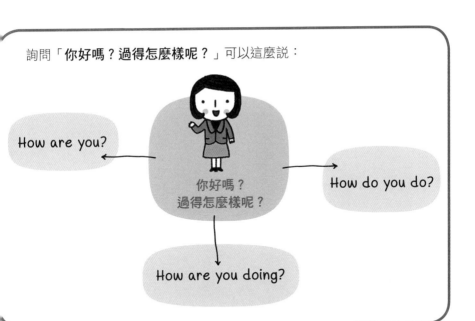

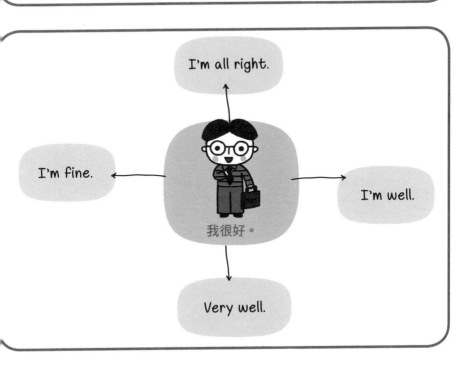

如果想回答「**很好！**」，並回問「**那你呢？**」，只需要在句尾加上「Thank you, and you?」就可以囉！

如果處在「**不太順遂的情況下**」或「**覺得不太好**」時，你可以回答：

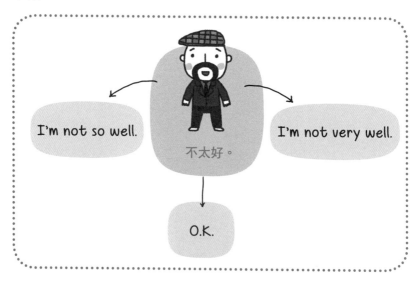

表示「**很高興見到你。**」或「**很高興能跟你聊天。**」你可以說：

很高興能見到你。

It's nice to see you.

I'm glad to meet you.

Pleased to meet you.

It's been a pleasure to meet you.

若要表示「**也很高興能夠見面。**」，則在句尾加上「**too**」就可以囉！

我也很高興見到你。

It's nice to see you, too.

I'm glad to meet you, too.

Pleased to meet you, too.

很高興能見到你本人。
（通常用於久聞對方名聲時的對話中）

It's nice to finally see you in person.

I'm glad to finally meet you in person.

I'm pleased to finally meet you in person.

「**告辭時**」，你可以說：

我必須先離開了。

I must leave now.

I must go now.

I must be on my way.

I'm afraid I'll have to go now.

和你聊天很愉快。

It's been a pleasure talking to you.

I've enjoyed meeting you.

It's been nice to talk to you.

如果你想回答「**我也覺得很愉快。**」或「**我也覺得和你聊天很有趣。**」在句尾加上「**too**」或回答「**Yes, it's been great.**」就可以囉！

Yes, it's been great.

表達「**希望能再次見面。**」可以說：

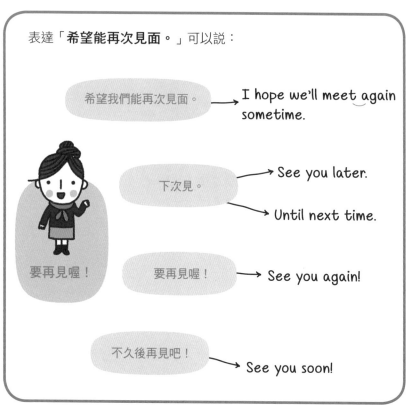

希望我們能再次見面。 → I hope we'll meet again sometime.

下次見。 → See you later.
→ Until next time.

要再見喔！ → See you again!

不久後再見吧！ → See you soon!

I'm sure we will.

I hope so.

我也希望能再次見面。

I hope so too.

把這些「**分別前的祝福用語**」都學起來吧！

Have a good trip.

Have a safe trip.

一路順風。

Bon Voyage.

Have a good time.

Have a good day.

祝好運。
祝愉快。

Have a nice holiday.

Have a good weekend.

假期愉快。

Take care of yourself.

Take care.

Take good care.

好好照顧自己。

祝好夢。

Sweet dreams.

祝好運。

Good luck.

Sleep well.

Sleep tight.

祝好眠。

「**告別時的用語**」還有哪些呢？

我們應該保持聯絡。

We should keep in touch.

We must keep in contact.

交換名片

Here's my card.
這是我的名片。

Here's my business card.
這是我的名片（比較完整的說法）。

Would you like my card?
您需要我的名片嗎？

May I give you my card?
我可以給您一張我的名片嗎？

你到這裡的時候打個電話給我吧！

Give me a call when you visit here again.

Why don't you give me a call when you're in town?

這些都是「**道別時**」的用語：

Goodbye.

再見。

Good-bye.

★ Goodbye 和 Good-bye 這兩種寫法都可以喔！

彼得·史密斯（Peter Smith）跟麗茲·沃登（Liz Wooden），他們因為生意而認識，但是不太熟識，兩人在機場巧遇……

Good afternoon, Ms. Wooden.
How are you?
午安，沃登小姐。妳好嗎？

Good afternoon, Mr. Smith. I'm very well. Thank you.
And you?
午安，史密斯先生。我很好，謝謝你，那你呢？

I'm all right. Thank you. It's nice to see you.
我很好，謝謝妳。很高興見到妳。

It's nice to see you, too. Well, I must be leaving now, or I'll miss my flight.
我也很高興見到你。嗯，我現在必須離開了，不然我會錯過我的班機。

It's been a great pleasure talking to you.
很高興能和妳聊天。

Have a good flight! I hope we'll meet again soon.
一路順風！希望我們很快能再次相見。

I hope so, too. Goodbye, Mr. Smith.
我也是。再見，史密斯先生。

Goodbye, Ms. Wooden. Until next time.
再見，沃登小姐。下次見。

柯提斯·凱博（Curtis Cabe）和潘·湯姆森（Pam Thomson）是曾一起工作的同事，偶然在市中心商業區巧遇……

Good morning, Ms. Thomson. How are you?

早安，湯姆森小姐。妳好嗎？

Good morning, Mr. Cabe. I'm fine. Thank you. And you?

早安，凱博先生。我很好，謝謝你。那你呢？

Very well. Thank you. It's been a great pleasure meeting you.

非常好，謝謝妳。很高興遇見妳。

Likewise. Well, I really must go now.

我也是。嗯，我現在真的必須走了。

All right. Have a good day!
好的。祝妳有美好的一天！

You too. We should keep in touch.
你也是。我們應該保持聯絡的。

Absolutely, we should. Why don't you give me a call when you're in town?
當然。妳到城裡的時候，何不打通電話給我呢？

Here's my business card.
這是我的名片。

Thank you. Here's mine.
謝謝你，這是我的（名片）。

It's been nice talking to you, goodbye, Ms. Thomson.
很高興能跟妳聊天，再見，湯姆森小姐。

It's been nice talking to you, too. Goodbye, Mr. Cabe.
我也很高興能跟你聊天。再見，凱博先生。

彼得・史密斯（Peter Smith）第一次和潘・湯姆森（Pam Thomson）
見面……

「How do you do?」是正式的招呼用語。「How do you do?」的回答不
是「你好嗎？」，我們可以用下列四種方式來回應：

❶ 回答「Hello.」

❷ 回答「I'm fine.」

❸ 以原來的句子回答「How do you do?」

❹ 如果是第一次見面，可以在原問句「How do you do?」的後方加上
「很高興見到你。」即：How do you do? It's nice to see you.

> **How do you do, Mr. Smith? My name's Pam Thomson.**
> 你好，史密斯先生，我的名字是潘・湯姆森。

> **How do you do, Ms. Thomson? It's nice to see you.**
> 妳好，湯姆森小姐，很高興見到妳。

非正式的招呼用語（Informal Greetings）

　　如果和很親密的人碰面，例如：朋友或熟識的人，我們可以用比較親切的方式來交談或稱之為「較不正式」的用語。

　　「**打招呼時**」可以這麼説：

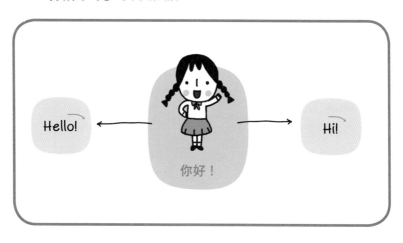

用來詢問「**你好嗎？過得怎麼樣呢？**」的用語有哪些？

一起來學習，回應「**過得怎麼樣呢？**」的非正式用語吧！

我很好。

I'm fine.

I'm good.

Fine.

Good.

Great.

O.K.

All right.

Couldn't be better.

還不錯，
不算太糟。

Not bad.　　Not too bad.　　Not so bad.

不太好。

I'm not
so well.

I'm not
very well.

Not so
well lately.

沒什麼特別。
普普通通。

Not much.　　Nothing much.　　Nothing special.

沒什麼，
老樣子。

So-so.

想告訴對方「**很高興見到你。**」可以這麼說：

用來詢問對方「**最近過得怎麼樣呢？**」的用語有：

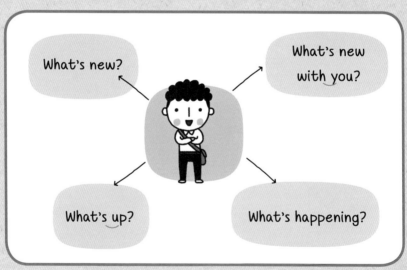

來學習「**說再見**」時的非正式用語吧！

說再見。

I'd better get going.

I've got to go now.

I have to go.

I'd better go now.

It's time to say goodbye.

當有朋友要「**告別**」時，我們可以用下列的句子來回應喔！

請隨意吧！

Don't let me keep you!
Go ahead!

噢，真的嗎？

Oh, really?

噢，這麼快就
要回去了嗎？

Oh, so soon?

別這麼急嘛！

Don't hurry off!

再多待一下
好嗎？

Can't you stay a little
longer?

「**分別**」時的用語，你知道的有哪些呢？

再見。／下次見。

See you.	再見。
See you soon.	不久後見。
See you later.	下次見。
See you again.	下次再相見。
I hope to see you soon.	希望很快能再相見。
I'll talk to you later.	下次聊。

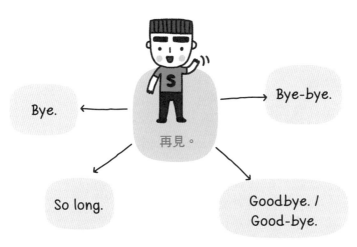

Bye.

Bye-bye.

再見。

So long.

Goodbye. / Good-bye.

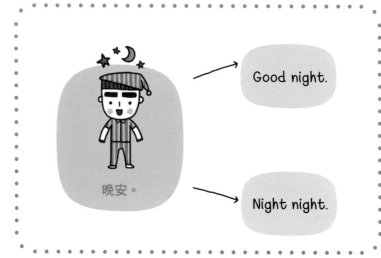

Good night.

Night night.

晚安。

生活會話「**超簡單**」 01-04

蘇珊·沃登（Susan Wooden）跟凱特·史密斯（Kate Smith）是很久沒見面的朋友，偶然間巧遇了……

Hi, Kate. How are you doing?
嗨，凱特。妳好嗎？

I'm good, thanks. And you?
我很好，謝謝。那妳呢？

Great! Nice to see you.

很好！很高興見到妳。

Nice to see you, too. What's new with you?

我也很高興見到妳，最近過得怎麼樣呢？

Nothing much. What about you? Long time no see.

普普通通，妳呢？好久不見了。

Yeah, it's been a long time. I've been so busy with school work these days.

真的，很久了呢！我最近都在忙學校的課業。

Anyway, I've got to go now. I'm late for class.

我現在要走了，上課快要遲到了。

Nice talking to you. See you later!

很高興能跟妳聊天，下次見！

Hope so. Bye-bye. Have a nice day!

希望如此，再見。祝妳有愉快的一天！

You too. Bye!

妳也是，再見！

圖解6到66歲都學得會的**超簡單英語會話**

佩特．絲莉南（Phetchama Srinam）跟威廉．摩根（William Morgan）很熟，偶然在某個午後於餐廳巧遇⋯⋯

Hello, Will.
How's it going?

哈囉，威廉。
你好嗎？

So-so, thanks.
And you?

普普通通，謝謝。妳呢？

Good. Glad to meet you.

很好，很高興見到你。

Glad to meet you,
too. What's up?

我也很高興見到妳。
最近過得怎麼樣呢？

Nothing special.
What about you?

沒什麼特別的。你呢？

Fine. I'm doing well,
actually.

很好，我最近過得不錯。

I've been working as an International Marketing Manager at ABC Company for a year.

我已經在 ABC 公司擔任一年的國際行銷經理。

Good for you! Well, I'd better get going. Nice talking to you.

太好了！嗯，我要先走了，很高興能跟你聊天。

Oh, really? Can't you stay a little longer?

真的嗎？妳不可以再多待一下子嗎？

I would like to, but I can't. I'm late for work.

我很想，但沒辦法。我上班要遲到了。

All right! See you soon. Take care!

好吧！不久後再見，好好照顧自己！

You too. See you!

你也是，再見！

Bye.

再見。

Chapter 2

第二章
嗨！我是丹尼爾·沃登。
Self Introductions

自我介紹時，該說些什麼呢？

我們想介紹自己讓他人認識時，例如：介紹自己給新同學、新同事，或者介紹自己讓客戶認識時，應該說些什麼呢？

說「你好！」

當然一開始都要先打招呼，向對方說聲「你好！」，接著才開始介紹自己，至於要跟一大群人自我介紹時，像是全班同學，或在正式的場合，跟重要客戶，就必須要用比較適當且有禮貌的開場白來介紹自己。

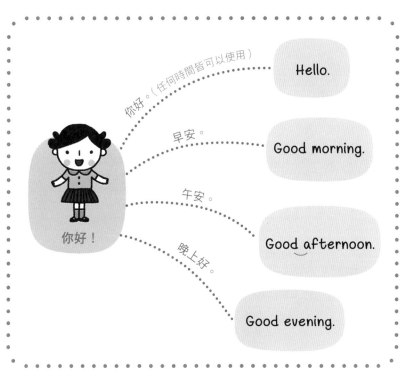

你好。（任何時間皆可以使用）　Hello.

早安。　Good morning.

午安。　Good afternoon.

晚上好。　Good evening.

你好！

Let me introduce myself.

May I introduce myself.

Allow me to introduce myself.

請容我自我介紹。

圖解6到66歲都學得會的**超簡單英語會話**

之後再繼續介紹「**姓氏**」、「**名字**」，並接著補充自己所屬的「**職位**」、任職的「**公司**」，或是自己正在就讀的「**學校**」……等。

> My name is + 名字、姓氏 + 職位、公司或學校

Good morning. Let me introduce myself.
My name is William Morgan from ABC
Company.

早安，請容我自我介紹。
我的名字是威廉‧摩根，來自 ABC 公司。

Good afternoon. May I introduce myself.
My name is Khanatda Smith.
I'm studying at Wan Suksa International
School.

午安，請容我自我介紹。
我是卡納姐‧史密斯。
目前就讀於日學國際學校。

Good evening. Allow me to introduce myself.
My name is Peter Smith, the president of
YOU Company.

晚上好，請容我自我介紹。
我是 YOU 公司的總裁彼得‧史密斯。

如果是在朋友間比較「**輕鬆的自我介紹**」，可以用親切一點的用語，不需要太過正式。

你好或抱歉 + 介紹名字、姓氏

Hello.
Excuse me.
Good morning.   } + I'm   + 名字、姓氏
Good afternoon.   My name is
Good evening.

Hello, I'm Susan Wooden.

Good afternoon. My name is Phetchama Srinam.

Excuse me. My name is Khanatda Smith.

在其他的自我介紹時，你也可以這麼說：

請問你的名字是……？

May I know your name, please?

Can you tell me your name, please?

Can I have your name, please?

我們之前認識或見過面嗎？
我們曾經見過嗎？

Have we met?

Have we met before?

Do I know you from somewhere?

Have we met somewhere before?

詢問「你是……對嗎？」
Are you + 名字、姓氏 + ?

Are you Mr. Smith?

Are you Ms. Wooden?

如果來不及聽清楚對方說的名字，我們可以禮貌地說下方的句子，讓對方再介紹自己一次。

I'm sorry. I didn't catch your name.

I'm sorry. What did you say your name was?

　　如果不確定是否可以直呼對方的名字或暱稱時，我們可以這樣詢問對方：

Can I call you + 需要稱呼的名字 + ？

Can I call you Peter?

Can I call you Dan?

在新年會上佩特察瑪・絲莉南（Phetchama Srinam）向彼得的太太瑪萊・史密斯（Malai Smith）介紹自己……

Good evening, Mrs. Smith.
I don't think we've met.
Let me introduce myself.

晚上好，史密斯太太。
我想我們之前還沒見過面。
請容我介紹自己。

I'm Mr. Smith's secretary.
My name's Phetchama Srinam.

我是史密斯先生的祕書。
我叫佩特察瑪・絲莉南。

It's been a pleasure meeting you in person, Phetchama.

很高興見到妳本人，佩特察瑪。

I've heard so much about you. Peter says you are a good secretary.

我聽了許多關於妳的事。
彼得說妳是一位很棒的祕書。

Thank you.
It's nice to finally meet you, too.

謝謝妳，很高興終於見到妳了。

麗茲・沃登（Liz Wooden）和瑪萊・史密斯（Malai Smith）之前並不認識，在一處宴會上坐在附近……

Hello. I don't think we have been introduced.

妳好，我想我們還不認識。

Allow me to introduce myself. I'm Elizabeth Wooden.

請容我自我介紹，我是伊莉莎白・沃登。

May I know your name, please?

請問妳的名字是……？

Hello, Ms. Wooden.
My name's Malai Smith.

妳好，沃登小姐，我叫瑪萊・史密斯。

Do I know you from somewhere?
我們之前在哪裡見過嗎？

Umm... are you Mr. Smith's wife?
呃⋯⋯請問妳是史密斯先生的太太嗎？

Yes, I am.
是的，我是。

It's good to meet you,
Mrs. Smith. I'm your husband's
friend.

很高興認識妳，史密斯太太。
我是妳先生的朋友。

Good to see you too,
Ms. Wooden.

我也很高興認識妳，沃登小姐。

肯‧史密斯（Khan Smith）介紹自己讓朋友們認識……

Hello, everybody. My name's Khanit Smith. But, please call me Khan.

大家好，我叫肯尼特‧史密斯，請叫我肯就可以了。

I'm English-Thai. I'm nineteen years old.

我是英泰混血兒，現在 19 歲。

I graduated from Wan Suksa International School.

我從日學國際學校畢業。

I'm glad to be here. Nice to meet you all!

很高興能來到這裡，並認識大家！

因為兩人在同一個社團裡，丹・沃登（Dan Wooden）跟肯・史密斯（Khan Smith）在第一次見面時，互相自我介紹……

Hi, I'm Daniel Wooden. What's your name?

嗨，我是丹尼爾・沃登。你叫什麼名字呢？

My name's Khanit Smith. But, you can call me Khan.

我叫肯尼特・史密斯，但你可以稱呼我肯就行了。

I'm sorry. I didn't catch your name.

抱歉，我剛剛沒聽清楚你的名字。

My name's Daniel. But, please call me Dan.

我叫丹尼爾，但請稱呼我丹就好了。

Nice to meet you, Dan.

很高興認識你，丹。

You too.

我也是。

Note

Chapter 3

第三章
很高興認識妳，
史密斯太太！
Other Introductions

介紹他人互相認識

我們時常需要介紹他人互相認識，好比介紹朋友之間認識、介紹不同的親戚或介紹同事之間認識……等。因此，必須學習在這些情況下該如何表達。

介紹他人互相認識的正式用語

如果要介紹認識的人是我們並不熟識、不親近的，例如：老師、教授、老闆、工作上的夥伴、顧客……等；在正式的場合上，好比會議中或與顧客的商談……等，必須使用比較正式的用語。

Let me introduce

May I introduce

Allow me to introduce

I would like to introduce

+ 名字、姓氏
彼此的關係
工作職位

介紹他人互相認識……

May I introduce my secretary, Miss Phetchama Srinam.

請容我介紹我的祕書，佩特察瑪‧絲莉南小姐。

Allow me to introduce Mr. Peter Smith, the president of YOU Company.

請容我介紹 YOU 公司的總裁，彼得‧史密斯先生。

I would like to introduce our International Marketing Manager, Mr. William Morgan.

請容我介紹我們的國際行銷經理，威廉‧摩根先生。

介紹他人互相認識的「半正式用語」

　　「**半正式用語**」是指沒有那麼正式，但仍算是比較有禮貌的說法，適用於比較熟識的人或用在不是非常正式的場合中，例如：聚會中、逛街或餐廳中巧遇⋯⋯等。

This is
I would like you to meet
+ 名字、姓氏
彼此的關係
工作職位

This is my wife, Malai Smith.
這是我的太太，瑪萊・史密斯。

This is a friend of mine,
Daniel Wooden.
這是我的朋友，丹尼爾・沃登。

I would like you to meet our
International Marketing Manager,
Mr. William Morgan.
我想讓你認識我們的國際行銷經理，威廉・摩根先生。

介紹他人認識的「非正式用語」

　　這種形式比較簡單，只要讓一方知道另一方的名字就可以，如同我們用中文介紹朋友們認識時也會說：「**丹，這是蘇珊。╱蘇珊，這是丹。**」

第 1 個人的名字 + meet + 第 2 個人的名字，
第 2 個人的名字 - 第 1 個人的名字
Dan, meet Susan, Susan-Dan.

Chapter 4

第四章
你的電話號碼是……？
Personal Data

詢問個人資訊

　　向他人詢問一些個人資訊時，有一些主要的問題是我們需要知道的，這些主要問題在英語中該如何呈現呢？讓我們一起來看看吧！

你叫什麼名字？	What is your name?
可以請你告訴我，你的名字嗎？（比較禮貌）	Can you tell me your name please?
你幾歲呢？	How old are you?
可以請你告訴我，你的年紀嗎？（比較禮貌）	Can you tell me your age please?

| 你來自哪一個國家／哪一個地區呢？ | Where are you from? |
| | Where do you come from? |

| 你是哪一國人呢？ | What is your nationality? |

| 你住在哪裡呢？ | Where do you live? |

| 你的地址是……？ | What's your address? |

| 你什麼時候出生的？ | When were you born? |
| | When is your birthday? |

| 你在哪裡出生的？ | Where were you born? |

| 你從事什麼工作呢？ | What do you do? |
| | What do you do for a living? |

| 你在哪裡工作呢？ | Where do you work? |

你的職位是……？	What is your position?
你在哪裡就學呢？	Where do you study?
你讀的是什麼科系呢？	What faculty are you studying in?
你的電話號碼是……？	What's your telephone number?
你的手機號碼是……？	What's your mobile phone number?
你有幾個孩子呢？	How many children do you have?
你有幾個兄弟姊妹呢？	How many brothers and sisters do you have?
你結婚還是單身呢？	Are you married or single?
你單身嗎？	Are you single?

凱特·史密斯（Kate Smith）和蘇珊·沃登（Susan Wooden）詢問彼此的電子郵件和手機號碼……

I have a very funny e-mail to show you. What's your e-mail address?

我有一封很有趣的信件想寄給妳看，妳的電子郵件地址是……？

My e-mail address is susanwoodens@hotmail.com What's yours?

我的電子郵件地址是 susanwoodens@hotmail.com，那妳的呢？

It's khanatdasmith@hotmail.com

（我的）是 khanatdasmith@hotmail.com。

By the way, I changed my mobile phone number.

對了，我的手機號碼換了。

It's 0982-149-823.

是 0982-149-823。

Hang on.
Let me save it.
等等，我存一下。

Tell me yours again, please.
請再告訴我一次，拜託。

0982-149-823. Got it?
0982-149-823。存好了嗎？

Yes. Thanks.
好了，謝謝。

What's your mobile
phone number?
妳的手機號碼是幾號呢？

I'll call you right now.
Got it?
我現在打給妳，有看到嗎？

Yeah, thanks.
有，謝謝。

肯・史密斯（Khan Smith）和丹・沃登（Dan Wooden）聊到彼此的科系和家庭……

What faculty are you studying in?

你唸哪一個科系呢？

I'm studying in the Faculty of Science and Technology.

我讀科學與科技系。

What is your major?

你主修什麼呢？

I'm majoring in Computer.

我主修電機。

What year are you in?

你幾年級？

I'm a freshman.

我是大一新生。

What do your parents do for a living?
你父母從事什麼工作呢？

**My dad is a businessman.
My mom is a housewife.**
我爸爸是商人，媽媽是家庭主婦。

How many brothers and sisters do you have?
你有幾個兄弟姊妹呢？

I have a younger sister.
我有一個妹妹。

What's her name?
她叫什麼名字？

Her name's Kate.
她叫凱特。

How old is she?
她幾歲呢？

She's 17.
她 17 歲。

佩特‧絲莉南（Phetchama Srinam）和威廉‧摩根（William Morgan）聊到彼此的家鄉和一些個人資訊……

Where are you from?
你來自哪裡呢？

I'm from England.
我來自英國。

Where do you come from?
那妳來自哪裡呢？

I come from France.
我來自法國。

What is your nationality?
你是哪一國人呢？

I'm English.
我是英國人。

Where do you live?
你住在哪裡呢？

I live in Taipei.
我住在台北。

Are you single?
妳單身嗎？

Yes, I am.
是的。

Where do you work?
妳在哪裡工作？

I'm working at YOU Company.
我在 YOU 公司工作。

What is your position?
妳的職位是？

I'm a secretary.
我是祕書。

Chapter 5

第五章
蘇珊有一雙褐色的眼睛。
Physical Appearance, Personality & Characteristics

形容他人的外表、人品和個性

我們時常會運用到與他人的外表、人品和個性有關的問句，例如：她的男朋友長什麼樣子？新的辦公室有什麼特色？入選大學新人之星的同學個性如何？與外表、人品和個性有關的各種句型，是我們這一章主要的學習內容。

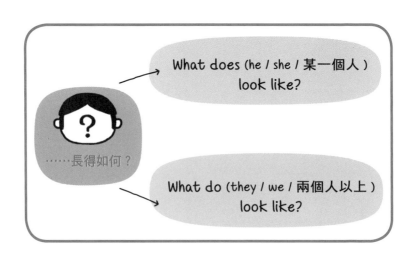

What is (he / she / 某一個人)
like?

What are (they / we / 兩個人
以上) like?

……個性如何？

What does she look like?
她長得怎麼樣？

What do Susan and Daniel
look like?
蘇珊和丹尼爾長得怎麼樣？

What is he like?
他的個性如何呢？

What are your parents like?
你父母的個性如何呢？

pretty	可愛的
beautiful	漂亮的
handsome	帥氣的
attractive	有吸引力的
good looking	長得很好看的
average	長得普通的

長相

straight hair	直髮
wavy hair	捲髮（波浪捲）
curly hair	捲髮
bangs	瀏海
braid	辮子
bun	圓髻
pony tail	馬尾
bald	禿頭
beard	濃密的鬍鬚
moustache	稀疏的鬍鬚

髮型

tall	高的
short	矮的
fat	胖的
chubby	圓胖的
plump	豐滿的
thin	瘦的
skinny	纖細的
well-built	體格很好的
fit	身材適中的

身高及體格

funny	有趣的
sociable	社交能力好的
good	好的
nice	棒的
kind	善良的
friendly	友善的
optimistic	樂觀的
easygoing	隨和的
diligent	努力的
reasonable	理性的
confident	有自信的

正向的個性

bad	糟糕的
shy	害羞的
quiet	安靜的
serious	嚴肅的
pessimistic	悲觀的
fussy	愛挑剔的
nosy	好管閒事的
selfish	自私的
foolish	愚蠢的
silly	傻呼呼的
stubborn	固執的
unreasonable	不理性的

負面的個性

How tall are you?
你多高呢？

....

How tall is (he / she / 某一個人)?
……多高呢？

How much do you weigh?
你幾公斤呢？

....

How much does (he / she / 某一個人) weigh?
……幾公斤呢？

What color are your eyes?
你的眼睛是什麼顏色的呢？

What color is your hair?
你的頭髮是什麼顏色的呢？

Do you wear glasses?
你有戴眼鏡嗎？

What color are her eyes?
她的眼睛是什麼顏色的呢？

What color is her hair?
她的頭髮是什麼顏色的呢？

Does that woman wear glasses?
那個女生有戴眼鏡嗎？

如果想問對方或別人的「**膚色**」，你可以這樣問：

詢問「**膚色**」對外國人來說是一件很敏感的事情。因此，這並不是一個會經常互相詢問的問題，也被認為是較為不禮貌的問題。如果真的必須要詢問的話，可以在句尾加上「**你的膚色是曬出來的嗎？（tan or fair）**」聽起來會比較有禮貌一些喔！

Are you tan or fair?
你的膚色是曬出來的嗎？

Is Pam tan or fair?
潘的膚色是曬出來的嗎？

膚色

white	白色的
fair	白偏黃的
dark	暗黑色的
tan	曬黑的膚色

瑪萊・史密斯（Malai Smith）問凱特・史密斯（Kate Smith）關於
蘇珊・沃登（Susan Wooden）的長相……

What does Susan look like?
蘇珊長得怎麼樣呢？

**She's quite pretty. She's medium
height and well-built.**
她很漂亮。身高中等而且身材適中。

**She has big brown eyes, short
straight blond hair and a
fair complexion.**
她有一雙很大的褐色眼睛、短直金髮
和淺色的肌膚。

凱特‧史密斯（Kate Smith）問蘇珊‧沃登（Susan Wooden）關於她哥哥的長相……

What does your brother look like?

妳哥哥長得怎麼樣呢？

He's average. He's tall and plump.

長得普通，他高高的而且微胖。

Does he have brown eyes and blond hair like you?

他有跟妳一樣的褐色眼睛和金髮嗎？

No, he doesn't. He has green eyes and short wavy brown hair.

不，他沒有。他有一雙綠色的眼睛和短的波浪捲髮。

丹·沃登（Dan Wooden）到肯·史密斯（Khan Smith）家舉辦的
生日宴會，有很多客人參加，丹詢問肯他的爸爸、媽媽是誰……

Which one is your father?

哪一位是你的爸爸？

He's the tall and fat man with short curly blond hair and green eyes.

他是那個高高胖胖的男人，有著金色捲髮和綠色眼睛。

Is he the man who has an oval face and a moustache?

是那個有鵝蛋臉和留著小鬍子的男人嗎？

Yes, that's right.

是的，沒錯。

How tall is he?
他有多高呢？

He's about 180 centimeters.
他大概 180 公分。

How much does he weigh?
他多重呢？

He weighs 80 kilograms.
他 80 公斤。

Which one is your mother?
哪一位是你的媽媽？

She's the tall and thin woman with long straight black hair and brown eyes.
她是那個又高又瘦的女人，有著長黑直髮和褐色眼睛。

Is she the beautiful woman who has a round face and a dark complexion?
她是那個圓臉且膚色比較深的漂亮女人嗎？

Yes. That's my mother.
是的，那個是我媽媽。

在同一場宴會上，蘇珊·沃登（Susan Wooden）問凱特·史密斯（Kate Smith）那些站在遠處但她不認識的人是誰……

Who is the woman wearing a black dress and a pair of red high heels?
那個身穿黑色禮服和紅色高跟鞋的女人是誰呢？

That's Phetchama, my father's secretary.
那是佩特察瑪，我爸爸的祕書。

What is she like?
她是個怎麼樣的人呢？

She's confident, easy-going and helpful.
她很有自信、隨和而且很會幫助別人。

She seems like a nice person.
她看起來是一位很好的人。

Yes, she is.
是，她是。

Which one is your brother?
哪一位是你的哥哥呢？

My brother is over there. See? He's the one wearing a striped shirt and jeans.
我哥哥在那裡，有看到嗎？
就是那個穿條紋襯衫和牛仔褲的人。

Is he the one wearing a pair of yellow sneakers?
他穿的是一雙黃色休閒鞋嗎？

Yes, he is.
是的。

He looks calm and quiet.
他看起來很安靜且木訥。

No, he isn't. Actually, he's quite funny.
不，並不是，其實他很有趣。

Chapter 6

第六章
不好意思，
你撥錯電話了。
Telephone Conversation

電話禮儀的須知

當我們是接電話的這一方，不管他人來電是因為工作需要、在家裡或私人電話，都有一些經常會運用到的說法，讓我們一起來看看有哪些吧！

接到「**正式電話**」時，例如：公務電話，你可以說：

你好＋介紹公司名稱＋需要什麼服務嗎？

Hello

Good morning   This is（地點名稱）
                    ＋   May I help you?
Good afternoon   Can I help you?

Good evening

正式電話的禮儀

Hello, ABC Company. May I help you?
你好，ABC 公司，有什麼需要服務的嗎？

Good morning.
This is International Marketing
Department. Can I help you?
早安，這是國際行銷部門，有什麼需要服務的嗎？

Good afternoon, Mr. Smith's office.
May I help you?
午安，史密斯先生的辦公室，需要什麼服務嗎？

「非正式電話」的禮儀

Hello.

Who is calling, please?

是誰打來的？

Who is speaking, please?

May I know who's speaking, please?

Who would you like to speak to, please?

詢問對方需要和誰通話

如果碰巧接到要找自己的電話，可以直接跟對方說：「**我正在聽，請講。**」

This is 自己的名字 speaking.

This is Dan speaking.

我正在聽，請講。

Speaking.

It's me.

當我們正在忙碌而不方便講電話時，可以跟對方說：「**等一下再回電。**」

我正在忙。

I'm in the middle of something. Can I call you back in a few minutes?
我正在忙，等一下再打過去好嗎？

Could you call back later?
你等一下再打過來好嗎？

如果來電者要求跟另一個人說話，我們可以跟他說：「等一下就為你轉接。」或「我（們）幫他找人過來接聽電話。」

One moment, please.

Just a moment, please.

請你稍等一下。

Hold on, please.

Hold the line, please.

Please hold the line for a few minutes.

我會為你轉接。

I'll put you through.

I'll get him for you.

我幫你找（某人）來。

I'll get... for you.

I'll get Mr. William for you.

I'll see if... is in.

我去幫你看看（某人）
還在嗎？

I'll see if she is in.

I'll see if Kate is in.

如果對方想找的人「**不在**」或「**沒空**」，用「**I'm afraid.**」或
「**I'm sorry.**」來向對方道歉是一種禮貌。

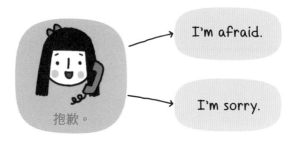

★ 道歉的句子要放在說明「對方不在」或「沒空」……等原因之前。

She'll be back in the afternoon.
她下午會回來。

He'll be back at 4 p.m.
他下午四點會回來。

「留言」或
「通知他人回電」

Would you like to leave a message?
你需要留個訊息嗎？

Can I take a message?
需要我幫你留個訊息嗎？

Can I have your name and number, please?
請讓我留下你的名字和電話號碼，好嗎？

I'll let (him / her) know when (he / she) gets back.
（某人）回來時，我會知會他／她。

打錯了嗎？沒有這個人。

I'm sorry. There's no one by that name.

抱歉，這裡沒有這個人。

I'm sorry. You must have dialed the wrong number.

對不起，你可能打錯電話號碼了。

I'm afraid you've got the wrong number.

抱歉，你可能撥錯號碼了。

撥打電話時的說法

　　至於，我們要打電話時，也會有一些不同的用法，讓我們一起來學習吧！

> 請求「與某人對話」
> 或請「對方轉接」

請找……

May I speak to + ..., please?

May I speak to Mr. Smith, please?

請找……

Could I speak to + ..., please?

Could I speak to Mrs. Wooden, please?

請找……

Can I speak to + ..., please?

Can I speak to Khun Peter, please?

請幫我找……

I would like to speak to + ..., please.

I would like to speak to Susan, please.

請幫我轉接到……

Could you put me through to...?

Could you put me through to the Sales Department?

那裡是……嗎？

Is that...?

Is that YOU Company?

介紹自己是誰

This is + 自己的名字 + from + 公司或辦公室的名稱 .

This is Elizabeth Wooden from ABC Company.

This is Peter Smith from YOU Company.

This is + 自己的名字 + speaking.

This is Curtis Cabe speaking.

This is Susan Wooden speaking.

This is + 自己的名字 .

This is Kate.

This is Dan.

Daily English Conversation

如果我們要找的人「**不在**」或「**不方便講電話**」，而我們需要「留訊息給對方」時，可以說：

請求留下訊息

Can I leave a message, please?

我可以留個訊息給他嗎？

Could you give her a message?

請幫我留個訊息給她，好嗎？

請告知回電

Could you please ask him to call me back?

請你轉告他，麻煩回個電給我好嗎？

Please tell him to call me back.

請告訴他回電給我。

Please tell her to call me back at...

請告訴她，在……時打電話給我。

告訴對方會再打來

That's O.K. I'll call back later.

沒關係，我會再打來。

When would be a good time to call you?

什麼時候方便打給你呢？

I'm sorry.
I dialed the wrong number.

抱歉，我打錯了。

打錯電話

關於「**其他撥打電話**」時的禮儀，你應該要知道的用法：

Can you speak up, please?

請大聲一點好嗎？

Could you speak a
little bit louder, please?

「漏聽」或「沒聽清楚」

Can you hear me clearly?
你聽得清楚嗎？

I can't hear you.
我聽不見你的聲音。

Your voice is very faint.
你的聲音很微弱。

I'm sorry, I didn't catch what you said.
抱歉，我沒聽到你剛剛說什麼。

I'm sorry, I didn't hear what you said.
抱歉，我剛剛沒聽見你說什麼。

可以再說一次嗎？

Can you repeat that?

Say it again, please?

佔線中

The line is busy.

The line is engaged.

沒有人接聽電話

No one answered the phone.

I'm sorry there's no one there at the moment.

凱特·史密斯（Kate Smith）打電話給蘇珊·沃登（Susan Wooden），蘇珊接到電話……

Hello.
你好。

Hello, can I speak to Susan, please?
你好，請找蘇珊。

It's Susan speaking. Who's calling, please?
我是蘇珊，請問是誰呢？

Hi, Susan. This is Kate.
嗨，蘇珊。我是凱特。

凱特・史密斯（Kate Smith）打電話給蘇珊・沃登（Susan Wooden），但是丹・沃登（Dan Wooden）接到電話，所以他去找蘇珊來接電話……

Hello.
你好。

Hello. Is that the Wooden's house?
你好，請問是沃登家嗎？

Yes, it is. Who would you like to speak to?
是的，請問你要找誰呢？

I'd like to speak to Susan, please.
請找蘇珊。

Who's speaking, please?
請問是哪位呢？

麗茲‧沃登（Liz Wooden）打電話找彼得‧史密斯（Peter Smith），但是彼得不在，是佩特察瑪‧絲莉南（Phetchama Srinam）接的電話，所以，她向麗茲詢問要留下的訊息……

Good afternoon, Mr. Smith's office.

午安，這是史密斯先生的辦公室。

May I speak to Mr. Smith, please?

請找史密斯先生好嗎？

I'm sorry. He's out for lunch. Would you like to leave a message?

抱歉，他出去吃午餐了。你需要留個訊息嗎？

Yes, please. Please tell him to call me back.

好的，請告訴他回電給我。

Can I have your name and number, please?

我可以留下妳的名字和電話號碼嗎?

I'm Elizabeth Wooden.

我是伊莉莎白‧沃登。

How do you spell your surname, please?

請問妳的姓氏怎麼拼呢?

W-O-O-D-E-N

W-O-O-D-E-N

W-O-O-D-E-N. And your phone number?

W-O-O-D-E-N,那妳的電話號碼是多少呢?

02-4443322.

02-4443322。

02-4443322.

02-4443322。

All right, Ms. Wooden. I'll let Mr. Smith know when he gets back.

好的，沃登小姐。史密斯先生回來時，我會轉告他。

Thank you. Goodbye.

謝謝你，再見。

Goodbye.

再見。

威廉·摩根（William Morgan）打電話找柯提斯·凱博（Curtis Cabe），但柯提斯正在電話中。因此，潘·湯姆森（Pam Thomson）請他稍等一下⋯⋯

Good afternoon,
Mr. Cabe's office.

午安，這是凱博先生的辦公室。

Good afternoon.
May I speak to Mr. Cabe, please?

午安，請幫我找凱博先生好嗎？

May I know who's
speaking, please?

請問是哪位呢？

William Morgan from
ABC Company.

我是 ABC 公司的威廉·摩根。

Hold the line, please.
I'll see if he's in.

請稍等一下，我去看看他在不在。

1 分鐘後

I'm sorry, Mr. Morgan. Mr. Cabe is on the other line.
很抱歉，摩根先生。凱博先生正在電話中。

Can you hold the line for a few minutes, please?
你可以稍待一會嗎？

Of course.
當然。

1 分鐘後

Hello, Mr. Morgan. Mr. Cabe is ready to speak to you now.
你好，摩根先生。凱博先生可以跟你通話了。

I'll put you through.
我為你轉接。

Thank you.
謝謝妳。

瑪萊‧史密斯（Malai Smith）要打電話找彼得‧史密斯（Peter Smith），但是撥錯電話了……

Hello.
你好。

Hello.
May I speak to
Mr. Smith, please?
你好，請找史密斯好嗎？

Sorry?
抱歉？

I'd like to speak
to Mr. Peter Smith,
please.
請幫我找彼得‧史密斯。

I'm sorry, there's no one by that name.
抱歉，這裡沒有這個人。

Is that YOU Company?
請問是 YOU 公司嗎？

No, sorry. This is ABC Company.

抱歉,不是的。這裡是 ABC 公司。

I'm sorry. I dialed the wrong number.

不好意思,我撥錯電話了。

That's O.K. Goodbye.

沒關係,再見。

Goodbye.

再見。

PART 2

Chapter 7

第七章
我們約幾點見面好呢？
Invitations & Appointments

邀請和約定行程

　　這個部分將從非常正式的邀約開始學習，例如：邀請他人到重要的典禮，好比說產品的發表會、擔任婚禮的見證人或邀請重要人士……等，都必須要非常有禮貌。

正式且有禮貌的邀請形式：

We would be very pleased if you could come to...

We would be very delighted if you could come to...

Would you care to come to...?

We would be very pleased if you could come to a grand opening ceremony for our latest products.

我們非常榮幸的希望能邀請你，蒞臨我們最新產品發表會的開幕典禮。

We would be very delighted if you could come to our company's charity auction.

如果你能蒞臨我們公司舉辦的慈善拍賣會，那真是我們的榮幸。

Would you care to come to our company's party this Sunday?

不知道你是否願意參加我們公司這個禮拜日舉辦的宴會呢？

說完之後，再補上一句「**謝謝對方的邀請。**」可以讓對方感覺到你的誠意喔！

謝謝你邀請我。

如果是「**不能赴約**」的情況，也有同樣禮貌且委婉地拒絕方式：

拒絕邀請

That's very kind of you, but + 理由

That's very kind of you, but I can't.
I have a meeting in the afternoon.
你真好，但是我沒辦法去。
我下午還有一個會要開。

That's very kind of you,
but I already have an appointment.
你真好，但是我已經有約了。

最後別忘了謝謝對方的邀請喔！

However, thank you for inviting me.
但還是謝謝你的邀請。

一般的邀約

　　瞭解禮貌的邀約形式後,來練習一下一般常用的邀約句子,
在正式或非正式的場合都可以使用:

提出邀請

Would you like to...?

I'd like you to...

Would you like to come to my birthday's party?
你要來我的生日派對嗎?

I'd like you to come to my birthday's party.
我希望你能來我的生日派對。

「接受邀請」
並「可以赴約」

Thank you.
I'd like to.

Yes, I would.
Thank you.

With pleasure.

「拒絕邀請」並表示「無法赴約」：

Thank you, but + 理由

I'm very sorry, I can't. + 理由

I'm terribly sorry, I can't. + 理由

> Thank you, but I have to work next Saturday.
>
> 謝謝你，但是我下個禮拜六要工作。

「拒絕邀請」
並表示
「無法赴約」

> I'm terribly sorry, I can't. I'm going to fly to Chiang Mai next week.
>
> 非常抱歉，我沒有辦法赴約。下個禮拜我要去清邁。

非正式的邀約形式

接下來要學習一些口吻比較親切的句子，好比邀約朋友或親近、比較熟識的人，我們會說「**去嗎？**」或「**一起嗎吧？**」來表達。

「去嗎？」、「一起去嗎？」、「有興趣一起去……嗎？」

Would you like to join...?

Do you want to join...?

Do you want to come...?

Why don't you join us...?

Do you fancy (動詞 ing)...?

Would you like to go to Kao Yai National Park with us next month?

下個月你有興趣跟我們一起去大山國家公園嗎？

Do you fancy seeing a movie with me on Sunday?

這禮拜天你有興趣跟我去看電影嗎？

Why don't you join us for dinner tonight?

今天晚上怎麼不跟我們一起吃晚餐呢？

All right.

O.K.

Of course.

「親切的」應答形式

Lovely.

Great.

I'd like to but I can't.
I have a stomachache.
我很想，但無法。
我肚子痛。

拒絕邀請

I'm sorry, I can't. I already
have plans. I'm going to meet
some old friends of mine on
Sunday.
很抱歉，我沒辦法去，我已經有計畫了。
我禮拜天要去見我的幾個老朋友。

約定時間常用的說法

約定時間 ....

What time would be most convenient for you?	你什麼時間最方便呢？
What time shall we meet?	我們幾點見面好呢？
What about (時間)?	（時間）好嗎？
How about (時間)?	（時間）好嗎？
About (時間)?	（時間）好嗎？

約定日期 ....

Does (日期) suit you?	（日期）你方便嗎？
Can you manage (日期)?	安排在（日期）你可以嗎？
What about (日期)?	（日期）好嗎？
How about (日期)?	（日期）好嗎？

回答對方提出的日期

Yes, that would be fine. 好的，這天有空。
Yes, (日期) is fine. 好，（日期）有空

Yes, Monday is fine.
好的，星期一有空。

Yes, Sunday afternoon is fine.
好的，星期天下午有空。

Yes, Tuseday at II is fine.
好的，星期二 11 點有空。

婉拒對方提出的日期

No, I'm sorry. ＋ 原因　　　　　不行，很抱歉＋原因

婉拒對方提出的日期

No, I'm sorry. I'm very busy on
Monday morning.

不行，很抱歉，我禮拜一早上很忙。

No, I'm sorry. I'll be away that day.

不行，很抱歉，那天我不在。

延至其他時間、日期

Can you manage Monday?
安排在禮拜一好嗎？

What about 11 o'clock?
11 點好嗎？

How about Sunday at 1 p.m?
禮拜天下午 1 點好嗎？

潘‧湯姆森（Pam Thomson）打給威廉‧摩根（William Morgan），
打算邀請他到公司的新產品發表會……

Hello. It's William speaking.
妳好，我是威廉。

Hello, Mr. Morgan. It's Pam Thomson.
你好，摩根先生，我是潘‧湯姆森。

Hello, Ms. Thomson.
How are you?
哈囉，湯姆森小姐，妳好嗎？

I'm very well. Thank you.
And you?
我很好，謝謝你。那你呢？

I'm good. Thank you.
我很好，謝謝妳。

Here's the thing, my company is going to have a grand opening ceremony
是這樣的，我們公司將舉辦一場開幕典禮，

for our latest products this Friday evening.
要發表我們的新產品，時間訂在禮拜五晚上。

We would be very pleased if you could come.
如果你能來參加，那將是我們的榮幸。

I'd very much like to. Thank you for inviting me.
我很高興，謝謝妳的邀請。

What time does the event start?
典禮幾點開始呢？

It starts at 5 p.m. at Splendid Hotel.
下午 5 點開始，在 Splendid 飯店。

I'll send you the invitation card in the afternoon.
我今天下午會將邀請卡寄給你。

Thank you. See you at the event.

謝謝妳，典禮上見。

See you there. Goodbye.

典禮上見，拜拜。

Goodbye.

再見。

佩特察瑪・絲莉南（Phetchama Srinam）打給麗茲・沃登（Liz Wooden）邀請她與彼得・史密斯（Peter Smith）商談新案子的事情……

Hello, Elizabeth speaking.
妳好，我是伊莉莎白。

Hello, Ms. Wooden. This is Phetchama phoning from YOU Company.
妳好，沃登小姐，我是 YOU 公司的佩特察瑪。

Mr. Smith from our company would like to meet you to discuss the new project both of you are doing together.
敝公司的史密斯先生想與妳見面商談新的案子。

Ah, yes.
啊，是的。

I'd like to arrange an appointment for him to meet you sometime next week at his office.
我必須幫他安排下個禮拜的某一天，在他的辦公室跟妳見面。
Does Tuesday suit you? About 9 o'clock?
禮拜二妳方便嗎？ 大概早上 9 點？
Er... let me check my schedule.
Umm... I'm afraid I'll be away that day.
呃……讓我確認一下我的行事曆。
嗯……那天我恐怕不在。
Can you manage Friday?
可以請妳安排在禮拜五嗎？
Certainly. What time would be most convenient for you?
當然，妳幾點方便呢？
How about 8 a.m.?
早上 8 點好嗎？

No, I'm sorry.
很抱歉。

Mr. Smith is having a meeting with the Sales Manager.
史密斯先生跟行銷經理有個會議。

Then what about in the afternoon?
Say 2 o'clock?
那下午呢？2點好嗎？

Yes, he's free then.
好的，他那個時間有空。

Lovely.
太好了。

Daily English Conversation

So it's 2 o'clock then on Friday the 12th at Mr. Smith's office.

那麼就決定是 12 號星期五，下午 5 點在史密斯先生的辦公室。

Yes, that would be fine. I'll confirm it with him.

好的，那太好了，我會告知他。

Thank you very much. Goodbye.

非常感謝妳，再見。

Great. I'm looking forward to it. Goodbye.

太好了，很期待這次的會面，再見。

凱特・史密斯（Kate Smith）邀蘇珊・沃登（Susan Wooden）去
Chatuchak Sunday 市場買東西，兩人在電話裡確定時間……

Hello.
妳好。

Hello.
Is that Susan?
妳好，是蘇珊嗎？

Yes, it's Susan
speaking.
是的，我是蘇珊。

Hi, Susan.
It's Kate.
嗨，蘇珊，
我是凱特。

Hi, Kate. How have you been?
I haven't heard from you for
a while.
嗨，凱特，妳好嗎？
我好久沒聽到妳的消息了。

I'm all right.
Thanks.
What about you?
我很好，謝謝妳。
那妳呢？

So-so.
Thanks.
普普通通，謝謝。

Are you free on Saturday?
如果禮拜六有空嗎？

Do you want to go shopping
at Chatuchak Sunday Market?
想不想去 Chatuchak Sunday 市場買東西呢？

I'm sorry, I can't. I already have an appointment
on Saturday.
很抱歉，我沒有辦法。我禮拜六已經有約了。

How about Sunday?
禮拜天好嗎？

Yes, Sunday's fine. Shall we say 9 o'clock?
好的，禮拜天也可以。我們早上 9 點見好嗎？

Yes, that's fine. Where shall we meet?
好，太好了。我們約在哪裡見面呢？

麗茲‧沃登（Liz Wooden）邀請彼得‧史密斯（Peter Smith）到
公司的宴會，但彼得要去紐西蘭，所以沒空⋯⋯

Hello, Mr. Smith.
你好，史密斯先生。

Hello, Ms. Wooden.
妳好，沃登小姐。

Would you care to come to our
company's party this Sunday?
你有興趣參加我們公司這禮拜天舉辦的宴會嗎？

That's very kind of you, but I'm flying
to New Zealand this Sunday.
妳人真好，但我這禮拜天必須飛去紐西蘭。

However, thank you for inviting me.
但還是謝謝妳邀請我。

That's all right.
沒關係。

Chapter 8

第八章
你的興趣是什麼呢？
Leisure Activities & Hobbies

詢問休閒活動及嗜好

　　詢問休閒活動、休閒時都做些什麼及嗜好，也是在進行會話時應該學會的主題，因為這是日常生活中經常有機會聊到的話題喔！

你休閒時喜歡做些什麼呢？

What do you do when you have some free time?

What do you do in your free time?

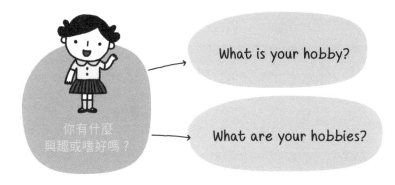

What is your hobby?

What are your hobbies?

你有什麼
興趣或嗜好嗎？

你多常……從事（某項活動）？

How often do you + 某項活動？

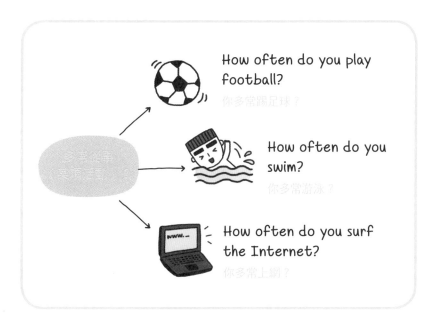

How often do you play football?

你多常踢足球？

How often do you swim?

你多常游泳？

How often do you surf the Internet?

你多常上網？

多常從事
某項活動？

SUN	MON	TUE	WED	THU	FRI	SAT
✓	✓	✓	✓	✓	✓	✓

Every evening.
每個晚上。

SUN	MON	TUE	WED	THU	FRI	SAT
			✓			

Once a week.
一星期一次。

SUN	MON	TUE	WED	THU	FRI	SAT
✓	✓	✓	✓	✓	✓	✓

Every single day.
每天。

SUN	MON	TUE	WED	THU	FRI	SAT
	✓		✓			

Twice a week.
一星期兩次。

SUN	MON	TUE	WED	THU	FRI	SAT
✓		✓		✓		✓

Every other day.
兩天一次。

SUN	MON	TUE	WED	THU	FRI	SAT
✓		✓		✓		

Three times a week.
一星期三次。

詢問「喜好」，你可以說……

What is your favorite + ...?

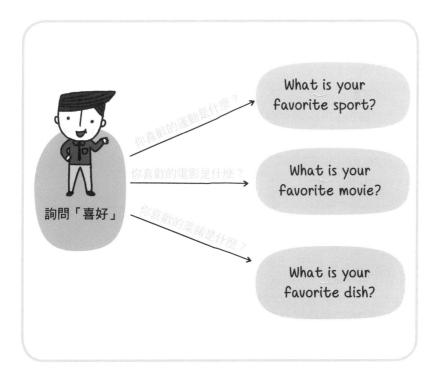

描述活動和體育時，使用「play」、「go」和「do」的文法

有注意到嗎？各式活動和體育常常使用動詞「play」、「go」和「do」，每一個的用法都各自不同：

1. 使用「play」的包括球類運動，或需要與其他人競賽的運動，包括足球、排球、網球和桌球……等。

playing sports	從事體育活動
playing golf	打高爾夫球
playing musical instruments	演奏樂器
playing badminton	打羽毛球
playing football	踢足球
playing chess	下棋

2. 去某個特定地點從事某項特定的活動時，必須使用「go」；同時，使用「go」的話，後方所連接的動詞後都必須加上「ing」，例如：

go shopping	去購物
go hiking	去爬山
go swimming	去游泳
go fishing	去釣魚
go windsurfing	去玩風浪板
go jogging	去慢跑

3. 很多休閒活動都可能會用到「do」，或是一個人進行而非
   團體活動的體育項目，例如：

doing crosswords   玩填字遊戲

doing jigsaw puzzles   玩拼圖

doing aerobics   做有氧運動

doing yoga   做瑜珈

doing karate   練空手道

doing gymnastics   做重量訓練

4. 其他的活動或體育項目，如下：

listening to music   聽音樂

watching movies   看電影

reading   閱讀

drawing   繪畫

surfing the Internet   上網

cooking   烹飪

singing   唱歌

taking photos   攝影

生活會話「超簡單」 08-01

蘇珊‧沃登（Susan Wooden）跟凱特‧史密斯（Kate Smith）聊到彼此的興趣……

What are your hobbies?
妳的興趣是什麼？

My hobbies are planting flowers, doing jigsaw puzzles and reading.
我的興趣是種花、拼圖和閱讀。

What kind of books do you read?
妳都看哪一類的書籍？

Short stories and novels.
短篇故事和小說。

Do you like reading novels?
妳喜歡看小說嗎？

I don't like to read.

我不喜歡閱讀。

I prefer watching movies.

我比較喜歡看電影。

What types of movies do you like?

妳喜歡看哪一類的電影呢？

I like thrillers.

我喜歡恐怖片。

Oh, I hate those. I love romantic comedies.

噢，我討厭恐怖片，我喜歡愛情喜劇。

What are your hobbies?

妳的嗜好是什麼呢？

I like doing yoga, swimming and playing chess.

我喜歡做瑜珈、游泳和下棋。

Do you play any sports?

妳有從事什麼運動嗎？

Not really. I'm not good at playing sports.

沒有，我對運動不在行。

Anyway, I like watching a tennis match.

但我喜歡看網球比賽。

So do I. We should watch it together sometimes.

我也是，我們改天應該一起看。

Good idea.

好主意。

佩特察瑪‧絲莉南（Phetchama Srinam）和威廉‧摩根（William Morgan）聊到彼此休閒的時候喜歡從事的活動……

What do you do in your free time?

你休閒的時候都會做些什麼呢？

In my free time, I like to play football, go fishing and play the guitar.

我空閒的時候喜歡踢足球、釣魚和彈吉他。

Play the guitar? Awesome!

彈吉他？真棒！

Thanks. What about you? What do you do in your free time?

謝謝，那妳呢？妳休閒的時候都在做什麼？

I like playing badminton,
doing aerobics and singing karaoke.
我喜歡打羽毛球、做有氧運動和唱歌。

I like to play badminton as well.
Do you want to play a match?
我也喜歡打羽毛球。妳想比賽一下嗎？

Good idea.
When's a good
time for you?
好主意，你什麼時候
方便呢？

I usually play after
work. How about
Wednesday evening?
我通常下班後打，禮拜三晚上
如何？

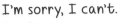

I'm sorry, I can't.
I'm busy.

很抱歉，沒辦法，我很忙。

I prefer the weekends.

我周末比較有空。

How about
Sunday evening?

禮拜天晚上呢？

Sure.
What time?

好，幾點？

5 p.m.

下午 5 點。

Great! I'll pick you
up at 4 p.m. on
Sunday.

太好了！我禮拜天下午
4 點去接妳。

Excellent!

太棒了！

Chapter 9

第九章
我喜歡義大利麵，
不喜歡炒年糕。
Likes & Dislikes

詢問喜歡或不喜歡

在生活中，如果你夠細心觀察的話，會發現我們在日常生活中常常會聊到喜歡或不喜歡什麼，例如：「我不喜歡吃青菜。」、「我喜歡日本料理。」、「我喜歡在工作的時候聽音樂。」或「我喜歡安靜地工作。」如何利用英文談論這些話題，其實是非常簡單的喔！

詢問「你喜歡……嗎？」

Do you like + 名詞？

Do you like + 動詞 ing？

Do you like+to + 原形動詞？

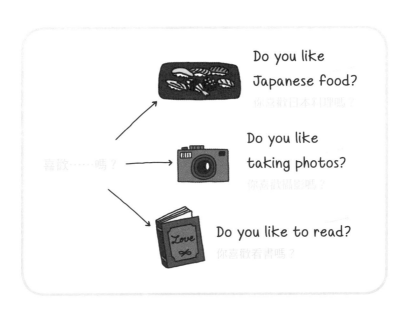

Do you like
Japanese food?
你喜歡日本料理嗎？

喜歡……嗎？

Do you like
taking photos?
你喜歡拍照嗎？

Do you like to read?
你喜歡看書嗎？

Yes, I do.
喜歡

No, I don't.
不喜歡

回答

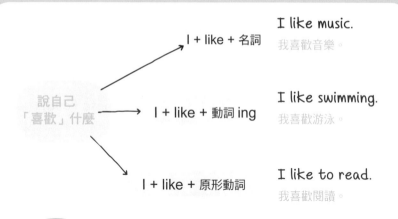

說自己「喜歡」什麼

I + like + 名詞
I like music.
我喜歡音樂。

I + like + 動詞 ing
I like swimming.
我喜歡游泳。

I + like + 原形動詞
I like to read.
我喜歡閱讀。

如果想表達「不喜歡」某些東西，則使用「don't like」。

說自己「不喜歡」什麼

I + don't like + 名詞
I don't like snakes.
我不喜歡蛇。

I + don't like + 動詞 ing
I don't like gambling.
我不喜歡賭博。

I + don't like to + 原形動詞
I don't like to work hard.
我不喜歡努力工作。

表達「也喜歡」的說法

　　如果有人說他喜歡什麼，例如：「**喜歡音樂**」或「**喜歡閱讀**」，而我們想表達自己「**也喜歡**」，可以使用「**too**」或「**as well**」。

我也喜歡。

I like it too.

I like it as well.

I like this restaurant.
我喜歡這間餐廳。

So do I.
我也喜歡。

Me too.
我也是。

表達「也不喜歡」的說法

　　至於，遇到有人說他「不喜歡」什麼，而我們也同樣「不喜歡」的時候，可以說「**Neither do I.**」或「**Nor do I.**」，即可表達「**我也不喜歡。**」的意思囉！

威廉·摩根（William Morgan）和潘·湯姆森（Pam Thomson）聊到彼此喜不喜歡韓國料理……

Do you like
Korean food?
妳喜歡韓國料理嗎？

Yes, I do.
我喜歡。

Would you like to have Korean
food for lunch with me tomorrow?
妳明天午餐想不想跟我去吃韓國料理呢？

Yes, I would. Thank you.
好啊，謝謝你。

By the way, I'm going to
see a play next Friday night.
對了，我下個禮拜五晚上要去看一場
話劇。

Do you like plays?

你喜歡看話劇嗎?

No, I don't. I prefer watching movies in a cinema.

我不喜歡,我比較喜歡去電影院看電影。

Do you like plays?

妳喜歡看話劇?

Oh, I love them.

噢,我很愛。

潘・湯姆森（Pam Thomson）和威廉・摩根（William Morgan）在
韓國餐廳裡，繼續聊著彼此喜歡和不喜歡的話題……

I like the food.

我喜歡這裡的料理。

Me too.
It's so delicious.

我也是，非常好吃。

But I don't
like the place.

但我不喜歡這間餐
廳。

Neither do I. It's too crowded.

我也不喜歡，人太多太擁擠了。

Besides, I think the waitress was rather rude.

而且，我覺得服務生很粗魯。

I don't like the way she talked and the way she treated us.

我不喜歡她跟我們說話和服務的態度。

I don't like the way she talked either.

我也不喜歡她講話的方式。

She should control her emotions.

她應該控制自己的情緒。

Chapter 10

第十章
你會游泳嗎？
Skills & Abillties

討論擅長和不擅長的技能

聊完喜歡和不喜歡的人、事、物……等話題之後，討論彼此擅長和不擅長哪些事情，也是日常生活中，跟朋友、同事……等，經常會談論到的話題。

你會……嗎？

你可以……嗎？

你能夠……嗎？

Can + you + 原形動詞？

Daily English Conversation

MP3 10-01

肯‧史密斯（Khan Smith）和佩特察瑪‧絲莉南（Phetchama Srinam）聊到彼此擅長與不擅長事情的話題……

凱特‧史密斯（Kate Smith）去蘇珊‧沃登（Susan Wooden）家玩，
聊到彼此會不會演奏樂器和游泳⋯⋯

> What's that?
> 那是什麼？

> It's the ukulele.
> 是烏克麗麗。

> Can you play it?
> 妳會彈嗎？

> No, I can't.
> But my brother can.
> 我不會，但我哥哥會。

Chapter 11

第十一章
我不同意你的看法。
Agreements & Disagreements

表達同意與反對

這一個部份我們要來學習表達意見的方式。需要特別注意的是，在英文句子中表示同意或反對時，句尾的語調如何變化，為本章的學習重點喔！

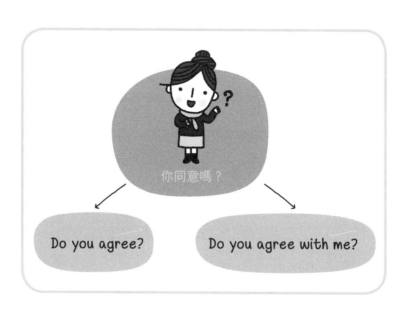

你同意嗎？

Do you agree?　　Do you agree with me?

你不同意嗎？

Don't you agree?   Don't you agree with me?

「同意」
請回答：
Yes, I do.

「不同意」
則說：
No, I don't.

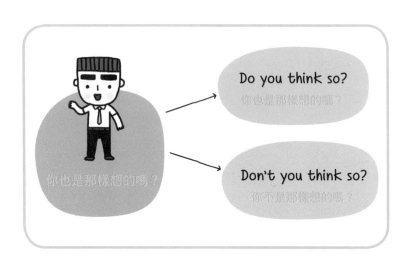

 I think this movie is fun.

我同意。

I agree.

I agree with you.

I think so.

我不同意。

I disagree.

I disagree with you.

I don't think so.

丹・沃登（Dan Wooden）和凱特・史密斯（Kate Smith）針對剛
剛看完的那部電影交換彼此的意見……

How was the
movie?

你覺得這部電影如何？

It was fun.

很有趣。

I agree.

我同意。

I like the action scenes.
They were exciting.

我喜歡動作的場面，很刺激。

Do you think so?

妳也這樣覺得嗎？

I'm sorry. I don't think so.
I think it sounded boring.

不好意思，我並不是那樣想的。
我覺得音樂聽起來蠻無聊的。

Anyway, I think we should see it
one more time.

總之，我想我們應該再看一次。

I'm sorry. I disagree.
Let's see another
movie next time.

抱歉，我不同意。我們下次
看別部片吧！

Chapter 12

第十二章
祝你好運！
Wishes & Congratulations

表達祝福的用法

這一章我們會先學習表達祝福的禮貌和正式用法，有哪些是你已經學習過的呢？有哪些又是你尚未接觸過的説法或用法呢？讓我們一起來看看吧！

我祝你……

I'd lke to wish you...

I wish you + 祝福的名詞或片語

接著，我們來學習一般較不那麼正式的用法：

I hope you have + 祝福的名詞或片語　　　我希望……

Have + 祝福的名詞或片語　　　祝你……

各種不同狀況的「**祝福語**」和「**祝賀詞**」：

All the best.
一切順利。

Good luck!
祝好運！

I'm glad to hear that.
我很高興聽到這個消息。

I wish you luck.
祝你好運。

Congratulations!
恭禧！

May all your wishes and
dreams come true!
希望你的願望和夢想都實現！

Congratulations on your marriage!
新婚愉快！

婚禮的祝賀語

Best wishes on your wedding.
祝você婚禮順利。

May your marriage bring you happiness.
祝福你的婚禮。

給病患的祝福

I hope you get better soon.

I hope you get well soon.

Get well soon!

Get better soon!

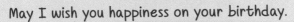

Congratulations on your success!
恭禧你成功了！

Congratulations on your promotion!
恭禧你升遷了！

Good luck on the job interview!
祝你面試順利！

I hope everything goes well
with your new job!
希望你新工作一切順利！

和「工作」
相關的祝福語

麗茲・沃登（Liz Wooden）禮貌地祝福輩分較大的彼得・史密斯
（Peter Smith）……

凱特‧史密斯（Kate Smith）祝福蘇珊‧沃登（Susan Wooden）
明天考試順利……

I'm having a math exam tomorrow.
我明天有個數學考試。

Good luck. I know you can do it.
祝好運。我相信妳辦得到。

Thanks a lot.
非常感謝妳。

丹・沃登（Dan Wooden）打電話給肯・史密斯（Khan Smith），
因為肯生病了沒去上學……

潘・湯姆森（Pam Thomson）祝佩特察瑪・絲莉南（Phetchama Srinam）生日快樂，佩特則祝潘旅途愉快……

Happy birthday, Phetch!
All the best!
生日快樂，佩特！
祝妳一切順心！

Thanks a lot.
非常感謝妳。

Are you and your family flying to Singapore tomorrow?
妳明天是不是要跟家人飛去新加坡？

Yes, we are.
是的。

Have a nice trip!
祝旅途愉快！

佩特察瑪・絲莉南（Phetchama Srinam）恭禧威廉・摩根（William Morgan）升遷了……

I just got promoted to the position of International Marketing Manager.

我剛剛升上國際行銷經理的位置。

Congratulations! You deserve it.

恭禧！這是你應得的。

Thank you. It's nice of you to say so.

謝謝，感謝妳的讚美。

Note

Chapter 13

第十三章

代我向彼得先生問好。
Please Say Hello to... / Send My Best Regards to...

寄託問候、思念及祝福

上一章學習完各類的「祝福語」，這一章的學習內容是向我們認識但無法見面的人「寄託思念」、「問候」和「祝福」，例如：朋友、爸爸、媽或朋友的親人……等，這些「問候語」在英文裡應該怎麼表達呢？

請代我向……表達思念之意：

Please give my regards to

Please give my best wishes to

} ＋ 該人的名字

寄託思念、祝福和問候的「非正式」說法：

Say hello to... for me.
代我向……問好。

Give my best wishes to...
代我祝福……。

Give my love to...
代我向……表達思念之意。

+ 該人的名字

寄託問候

Say hello to your brother for me.
代我向你哥哥問好。

Give my best wishes to Dan.
代我問候丹。

Give my love to Kate and Khan.
幫我跟凱特和肯說我很想念他們。

麗茲‧沃登（Liz Wooden）問候彼得‧史密斯（Peter Smith）的
太太……

How is your wife?
你太太最近過得怎麼樣呢？

She's fine.
她很好。

Please give my
regards to her.
代我向她問好。

All right, I will.
好，我會的。

蘇珊‧沃登（Susan Wooden）問候凱特‧史密斯（Kate Smith）
的哥哥……

Say hello to your
brother for me.
代我向你哥哥問好。

O.K., I will.
好，我會的。

潘·湯姆森（Pam Thomson）請佩特察瑪·絲莉南（Phetchama Srinam）問候其他的朋友們……

Jen, Tom and I are going
to visit Pattaya this Sunday.
珍、湯姆和我這禮拜天要去 Pattaya。

Would you like to go with us?
妳想跟我們去嗎？

I'd love to, but I can't.
I'm busy.
我很想，但沒辦法，我很忙。

Please give my love to
Jen and Tom.
請代我跟珍和湯姆問好。

丹‧沃登（Dan Wooden）問候肯‧史密斯（Khan Smith）的
媽媽⋯⋯

Note

Chapter 14

第十四章
別放棄，
下次會更好運的！
Regret & Sympathy

表達「遺憾」或「同情」，你可以說……

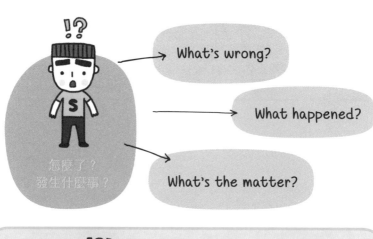

What's wrong?

What happened?

What's the matter?

怎麼了？
發生什麼事？

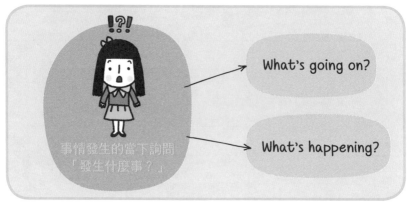

What's going on?

What's happening?

事情發生的當下詢問
「發生什麼事？」

表達「遺憾」和「同情」

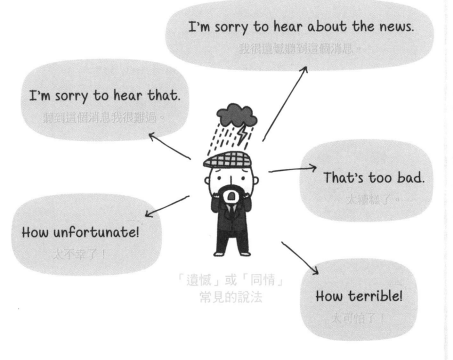

表達對「逝世」的遺憾與「同情（人或寵物）」

I'm sorry for your loss.
對你失去的一切，我感到很遺憾。

My condolences to you and your family.
你和家人的悲傷，我感同身受。

對「考試沒通過」表達遺憾之意

I'm sorry that you didn't pass the exam.
很遺憾，你沒有通過那個考試。

I'm sorry to hear that you failed the test.
聽到你考試沒通過，我很難過。

Better luck next time!
下次會更好運的！

I'm sorry to hear about the difficulties you've faced.

我很遺憾，聽到你最近過得不太好。

I'm sorry to hear that you're having a hard time.

聽到你最近過得不太好，我很難過。

如果有什麼需要幫忙的，就說吧！

If there is anything I can do for you, let me know!

凱特·史密斯（Kate Smith）對蘇珊·沃登（Susan Wooden）逝世的祖母表達遺憾之意……

What's wrong, Susan?
You look really sad.

怎麼了，蘇珊？妳看起來很難過。

My grandmother passed away
last night.

我奶奶昨晚過世了。

I'm sorry for your loss.

對妳失去的一切，我感到很遺憾。

丹‧沃登（Dan Wooden）向考試沒過的肯‧史密斯（Khan Smith）
打氣……

What's wrong?
You seem upset.
怎麼了？你看起來很沮喪。

I failed the math exam.
我沒通過數學考試

Don't give up!
Better luck next time.
別放棄！下次會更好運的

潘‧湯姆森（Pam Thomson）對遺失手機的丹‧沃登（Dan Wooden）表達同情之意……

What happened?
怎麼了？

I've lost my mobile phone at the shopping mall.
我的手機在購物中心弄丟了。

Oh! That's too bad.
噢！真糟糕。

佩特察瑪・絲莉南（Phetchama Srinam）向弟弟出車禍的威廉・摩根（William Morgan）表達同情……

What's the matter?
You look so worried.

怎麼了嗎？你看起來很擔心。

My brother had a car accident last night.

我弟弟昨晚出車禍。

I'm sorry to hear that. How is he?

很遺憾聽到這個消息。他還好嗎？

He's at the hospital.
He broke his arm.

他在醫院裡，手臂骨折了。

How terrible! I hope he gets better soon!

太可怕了！希望他快點好起來！

Thank you.

謝謝妳。

Chapter 15

第十五章
多美的洋裝啊！
Giving Praise

稱讚他人和回應讚美

　　有沒有想過該如何讚美他人呢？在這一章的學習內容中，我們將會學習到各種稱讚他人的句子，例如：「你真好。」、「妳真漂亮。」或「你好聰明。」……等。這些讚美的話語，在英文中的説法及用法，其實是非常簡單的。

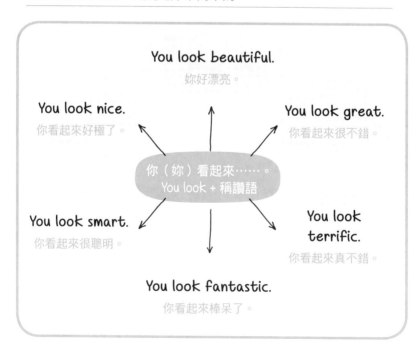

You look beautiful.
妳好漂亮。

You look nice.
你看起來好極了。

You look great.
你看起來很不錯。

你（妳）看起來……。
You look + 稱讚語

You look smart.
你看起來很聰明。

You look terrific.
你看起來真不錯。

You look fantastic.
你看起來棒呆了。

如果想強調稱讚的事情，例如：「**你看起來非常漂亮。**」、「**你人真的很好。**」。在英文句子中，「非常」可以用「**very**」來表達，至於「真的」則是用「**really**」喔！

You look + very + 稱讚語
你看起來非常……。

You look very beautiful.
妳看起來非常漂亮。

You look very nice.
你看起來非常好。

You look + 稱讚語 + really
你看起來真的很……。

You look different, really.
你看起來真的很不一樣。

You look smart, really.
你看起來真的很聰明。

「稱讚物品」時，可以運用下列的句型來表達：

That's　+　a nice　　　　　+　「東西」或「物品」

That's　+　a beautiful　　　+　「東西」或「物品」

That's　+　a perfect　　　　+　「東西」或「物品」

That's　+　a very nice　　　+　「東西」或「物品」

That's　+　a very beautiful　+　「東西」或「物品」

That's a very nice car.
那是一台非常棒的車。

That's a perfect watch.
那是一支非常棒的手錶。

稱讚物品

That's a beautiful garden.
那是一座很漂亮的花園。

That's a very beautiful
mobile phone.
那是一支很漂亮的手機。

　　除了這些常用的說法之外，你也可以運用含有「讚嘆語氣」
的讚美，例如：「**多美啊！**」、「**真的是太厲害啦！**」、「**太
可愛啦！**」……等，這些「讚嘆語氣」的讚美句子，在英文中也
有不一樣的用法喔！

How + 用以稱讚的（形容詞）+ 代名詞 + 動詞

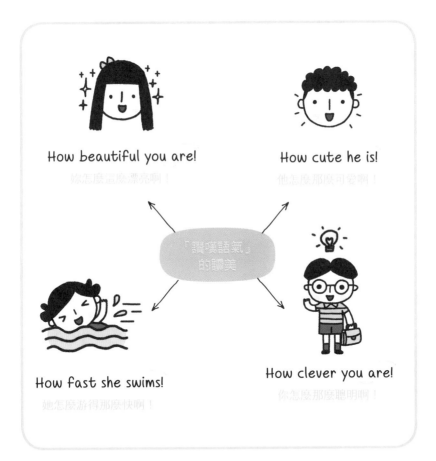

How beautiful you are!
你怎麼這麼漂亮啊！

How cute he is!
他怎麼那麼可愛啊！

「讚嘆語氣」
的讚美

How fast she swims!
她怎麼游得那麼快啊！

How clever you are!
你怎麼那麼聰明啊！

What a beautiful skirt!

多美的裙子啊！

What a good idea you have!

你怎麼有那麼好的點子啊！

What a smart kid he is!

多麼聰明的孩子啊！

What a pretty lady she is!

多麼美麗的女士啊！

彼得・史密斯（Peter Smith）稱讚瑪萊・史密斯（Malai Smith）
今天很漂亮……

You look beautiful today!
妳今天好漂亮！

Thank you for your compliment.
You're so sweet.
謝謝你的讚美，你嘴真甜。

佩特察瑪・絲莉南（Phetchama Srinam）稱讚威廉・摩根
（William Morgan）的衣服……

What a nice T-shirt!
好棒的 T 恤啊！

Thanks. I'm glad you
think so.
謝謝，很高興妳也這麼想。

柯提斯‧凱博（Curtis Cabe）稱讚潘‧湯姆森（Pam Thomson）
的新髮型……

Did you have a new
hair cut?

妳換新髮型嗎？

Yes, I did.

是的。

Wow! I like your new
hair style.

哇！我喜歡妳的新髮型。

You look very different and a
lot younger.

妳看起來很不一樣，而且更年輕了。

I appreciate the compliment.
I'm glad you like it.

謝謝你的讚美，很高興你喜歡。

Chapter 16

第十六章
謝謝你的建議。
Expressing Gratitude

「表達感謝」也是生活中經常遇到的情境。有沒有試著想過，在一天當中，我們對他人會說幾次「謝謝」呢？所以，我們應該來學習如何表達謝意的說法，讓自己成為更有禮貌的人喔！

表達感謝

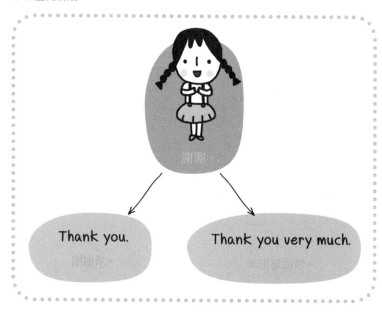

謝謝

Thank you.
謝謝你。

Thank you very much.
非常感謝你。

「感謝」特定的某件事情

Thank you for + 要「感謝」的事情

Thank you for your help.
謝謝你的幫助。

Thank you for your kindness.
謝謝你的善意。

Thank you for your suggestion.
謝謝你的建議。

Thank you for your advice.
謝謝你的勸告。

Thank you for everything.
謝謝你提供的一切。

各種不同「表達感謝」的說法

在英文中，除了「Thank you.」還有其他很多種表達感謝的說法喔！

各種不同「表達感謝」的說法

Much appreciated.

You're so kind!

I really appreciate that.

How kind of you!

I appreciate your help.

That's very kind of you.

That's very nice of you.

「回應感謝」的說法

You're welcome.

You're most welcome.

My pleasure.

It was my pleasure

Don't mention it.

No problem.

Not at all.

Any time.

佩特察瑪・絲莉南（Phetchama Srinam）搬很重的東西，威廉・摩根（William Morgan）幫了她一把……

Oh! It's so heavy.

噢！好重。

Let me help you.

讓我來幫妳。

Thank you for your help.

謝謝你的幫忙。

Any time.

不客氣。

Note

丹‧沃登（Dan Wooden）謝謝肯‧史密斯（Khan Smith）借他
錢……

Can I borrow you some money,
please?
我可以跟你借點錢嗎？

Yes, you can.
How much money do you
want?
好的。你需要多少呢？

500 dollars.
500 塊。

Here you are.
這裡。

Thank you for your
kindness.
謝謝你的幫忙。

You're welcome.
不客氣。

Chapter 17

第十七章
請原諒我。
Apologies

表達歉意

　　學會用英文表達「感謝」之外，學習真誠的「道歉」也是生活中重要的一環喔！現在腦海中，有沒有閃過哪些常會用到的「道歉」形式呢？（有的話，請別每天都在道歉啊！）。如果尚未想到，沒關係！我們馬上來學一下「道歉」和「請求原諒」在英文中該如何表達，一起來看看吧！

I'm sorry.
對不起。

I do apologize.
抱歉。

Please forgive me.
請原諒我。

對不起。
（在各種情況下都可以使用）

Please accept my apology.
請接受我的道歉。

對已經做出的事情
表達「歉意」

I'm sorry for my mistake.

我對我犯下的錯誤感到抱歉。

I'm sorry for what I have done.

我對我做的事情感到抱歉。

I'm sorry. I didn't mean to do those things to you.

我很抱歉，我不是故意要對你做那些事的。

I'm so sorry. It's my fault.

非常抱歉，都是我的錯。

I'm sorry for being late.

對不起，我遲到了。

Sorry, I'm late.

對不起，我遲到了。

Sorry, I kept you waiting.

對不起，讓你久等了。

Sorry for the delay.

對不起，我來晚了。

I'm sorry that I hurt your feelings.

傷了你的感覺，我很抱歉。

I'm sorry that I hurt you.

很抱歉傷了你。

I'm sorry. I didn't mean to say bad things to you.

很抱歉，我不是故意要跟你說那些難聽的話。

I can't tell you how sorry I am.

我沒辦法跟你說我有多愧疚。

I'm sorry that I lost my temper.

很抱歉，我情緒失控了。

「回應道歉」時，你可以說：

That's all right.　　　　It's O.K.

沒關係。

That's O.K.

It's all right.

It doesn't matter.

I accept your apology.

Don't worry about it.

Let's forget it.　　It wasn't your fault.

Daily English Conversation

丹‧沃登（Dan Wooden）走路不小心撞到肯‧史密斯（Khan Smith）……

瑪萊‧史密斯（Malai Smith）因為之前的爭吵，跟彼得‧史密斯
（Peter Smith）道歉……

I'm sorry that I lost my temper.
很抱歉，我情緒失控了。

I know you didn't mean it.
Let's forget it!
我知道妳不是有心的，忘了吧！

威廉‧摩根（William Morgan）因為遲到，跟潘‧湯姆森（Pam Thomson）道歉……

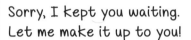

Sorry, I kept you waiting.
Let me make it up to you!
對不起，讓妳久等了。
讓我補償你吧！

I'll buy you dinner
tonight.
我今晚請你吃晚餐。

You don't have to!
不用這樣啦！

I insist!
就讓我請吧！

Well, O.K! if you insist.
嗯，好吧！如果你堅持的話。

佩特察瑪‧絲莉南（Phetchama Srinam）因為送錯文件跟彼得‧史密斯（Peter Smith）道歉……

I think you've given me the wrong file.

我想妳拿錯文件給我了。

I do apologize, sir.

很抱歉，先生。

It doesn't matter.

沒關係。

Please give me the right one.

請拿對的那一份給我。

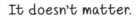

I'll go and get it right away, sir.

我馬上送過去，先生。

圖解6到66歲都學得會的**超簡單英語會話**

Chapter 18

第十八章
你應該要去運動一下。
Suggestions

關於建議的用法

　　當你想給他人建議時，你會如何表達呢？無論是在研討課業、工作場合、買賣購物……等，任何場合都可能會運用到「提供建議」的說法，不學起來怎麼可以呢！準備好了嗎？要開始進入這一章囉！

> 你應該……。
> **You should + 動詞**
>
> 你最好……。
> **You'd better + 動詞**
>
> 你為什麼不……呢？
> **Why don't you + 動詞 + ...?**

Tips:「'd better」是「had better」的縮寫，要記得喔！

You should get some sleep.
你應該去睡一下。

You should see the dentist.
你應該要去看牙醫。

You'd better get some rest.
你最好休息一下。

You'd better see the doctor.
你最好去看個醫生。

Why don't you
sit down and relax?
你為什麼不坐下來放鬆一下呢？

Why don't you have some food?
你為什麼不吃一點東西呢？

「回應建議」時，你可以說：

I think so.
我也是這麼想的。

That's a good idea.
好主意。

Maybe I should.
也許我應該這麼做。

I think you're right.
我想你是對的。

You're absolutely right.
你說的對極了。

Maybe you're right.
也許你是對的。

彼得‧史密斯（Peter Smith）剛從公司回來，看起來累壞了。
瑪萊‧史密斯（Malai Smith）建議他要好好照顧自己……

I don't know what's wrong with me.
我不知道怎麼了。

I usually feel exhausted all day long.
常常覺得整天都好累。

You'd better get some exercise.
你最好去做些運動。

And sometimes I can't sleep at night.
而且，有的時候我晚上都睡不著。

I think you're working too hard.
我想你工作太勞累了。

You should take a few days off.
你應該放幾天假。

Maybe I should.
也許我應該這麼做。

肯‧史密斯（Khan Smith）剛剛運動回來，瑪萊‧史密斯（Malai Smith）建議他先洗個澡⋯⋯

I'm so tired and hungry.
我好累而且好餓。

Why don't you have a shower, eat some sandwiches and rest?
你為什麼不先洗個澡、吃點三明治，再去休息一下呢？

That's a good idea, Mom.
媽媽，這真是個好主意。

凱特·史密斯（Kate Smith）肚子痛，瑪萊·史密斯（Malai Smith）建議她去看醫生……

I have a terrible stomachache.
我肚子好痛。

You'd better see a doctor.
妳最好去看個醫生。

Yes, I think so.
對，我也這麼想。

I'll take you to the hospital.
我帶妳去醫院。

Thank you, mom.
謝謝，媽媽。

Chapter 19

第十九章
沃登小姐，
妳需要喝點什麼嗎？
Making an Offer

「提供服務」的正式用法

　　常聽到「提供服務」的說法，像是「來杯咖啡好嗎？」、「要試看看嗎？」、「要品嚐一下嗎？」……等。這些簡單的詢問，該如何用英文表達呢？這一章將從正式且有禮貌的用法開始介紹，好比詢問客人「要不要點杯咖啡？」之類的說法。

> 需要……嗎？
>
> Could I offer you...?
>
> Would you care for...?

Could I offer you a glass of lemonade?

需要我幫你點杯檸檬汁嗎？

Would you care for a piece of chocolate cake?

你想要點一塊巧克力蛋糕嗎？

「提供服務」的「一般」說法

在不是非常正式的場合裡，我們可以用下列這些句子：

要喝點什麼呢？

What would you like to drink?

What can I get you?

你需要……嗎？

Can I offer you...?

Would you like...?

Can I offer you a glass of water?

我幫你拿杯水好嗎？

Would you like some vanilla ice cream?

你想要來一點香草冰淇淋嗎？

「提供服務」的「非正式」說法

如果我們是為「**朋友**」或「**熟識**」的人「**提供服務**」時，我們可以用比較輕鬆的語氣，就像在我們常常會用「**要水嗎？**」或「**要咖啡嗎？**」……等說法。

「回應提供服務」的句子

如果有人要為我們提供服務，我們「**很樂意接受**」時，可以這麼回答：

「婉拒」服務

相反地，如果我們「**不需要**」對方的服務時，你可以運用下方的句子來婉拒：

彼得・史密斯（Peter Smith）和麗茲・沃登（Liz Wooden）在談公事，佩特察瑪・絲莉南（Phetchama Srinam）來詢問兩人需要喝點什麼……

Excuse me, what would you like to drink, Mr. Smith?

抱歉，史密斯先生，你需要喝點什麼嗎？

A cup of coffee, please. Thank you.

請給我一杯咖啡，謝謝。

What can I get you, Ms. Wooden?

我可以為妳點些什麼呢？沃登小姐。

A cup of tea for me, please.
Thank you.
請給我一杯茶，謝謝妳。

Here you are.
請用。

5 分鐘後

Thank you very much.
非常感謝妳。

Please let me know if you need anything else.
如果兩位還需要什麼，請跟我說。

I will. Thank you.
好的，謝謝妳。

1個小時後，佩特察瑪・絲莉南（Phetchama Srinam）覺得茶飲應該沒了，所以過來詢問兩人是否需要續杯……

I'm sorry to interrupt.
抱歉，打擾了。

I wonder if I might give you another cup of coffee, Mr. Smith.
我想我可以再幫你倒杯咖啡，史密斯先生。

Yes, please.
好的。

Would you care for another cup of tea, Ms. Wooden?
妳需要再來杯茶嗎？沃登小姐。

That would be very nice.
那太好了。

凱特・史密斯（Kate Smith）邀蘇珊・沃登（Susan Wooden）
到家裡玩，瑪萊・史密斯（Malai Smith）出來歡迎她……

Would you like a glass of orange juice?
妳要來杯橘子汁嗎？

Yes, please.
好的。

Just one moment. I'll be right back.
等一下，很快就好了。

Here you go.
請用。

Have some cookies, Susan.
吃點餅乾，蘇珊。

3 分鐘後

Thank you, Mrs. Smith.
謝謝妳，史密斯太太。

Make yourself at home!
把這裡當自己家喔！

Note

Chapter 20

第二十章
我可以請幾天假嗎？
Asking for Permission

徵求同意的說法

　　「徵求同意」是學習英文的另一個重點。當我們在公共場合或有其他人在場的時候，想要做些什麼事情之前，應該都要先詢問他人或徵求對方的同意。這些用法，都會囊括在這一章裡面喔！

> 我可以⋯⋯嗎？
>
> Can I + 動詞？
>
> Could I + 動詞？
>
> May I + 動詞？
>
> ★ 「could」通常置於句首，是比較禮貌且稍微正式一點的用法；相反的，用於熟識的人之間，則可以將「can」置於句首即可。

Can I use your phone for a few minutes?
我可以用一下你的手機嗎？

Can I sit here?
我可以坐在這裡嗎？

Could I borrow your pen, please?
請問我可以借用一下你的筆嗎？

Could I have a glass of water?
我可以要一杯水嗎？

May I come in, please?
請問我可以進來嗎？

May I ask you a personal question?
我可以問你一個問題嗎？

「徵求同意」的回應

Yes.	好。
Sure.	當然。
Go ahead.	儘管去做。
Certainly.	當然。
Of course.	當然。
O.K.	好的。
All right.	好。
No problem.	沒問題。

「不認同」時，可以說……

No, I'm sorry. ＋原因

I'm afraid you can't. ＋原因

I'm afraid you couldn't. ＋原因

I'm afraid you may not. ＋原因

No, I'm sorry. I'm using it.
不行，很抱歉，我正在使用。

I'm afraid you can't.
I'm using it tomorrow.

很抱歉，真的沒辦法，我明天會用到。

你介意，我……嗎？

Do you mind if I + 原形動詞？

Would you mind if I + 過去式動詞？

你介意我在這裡抽菸嗎？

Do you mind if I smoke here?

Would you mind if I smoked here?

你介意我把電視的聲音轉小聲嗎？

Do you mind if I turn down
the TV?

Would you mind if I turned down
the TV?

回應「不介意」

　　以「Do you mind...?」或「Would you mind...?」開始的問句，是想知道對方心中的感受，有「**如果我這樣做的話，對方會介意嗎？**」的想法。因此，如果你想允許對方做某件事，必須回答「**不介意**」即「No.」，給予許可的回答；如果回應「Yes.」則表示「**介意**」，有不允許的意思。

「不允許」時，可以說……

Yes, I do. + 不允許的理由

Yes, I would. + 不允許的理由

Yes, I do. This is a non-smoking room.
是的，我介意，這裡是禁菸區。

Yes, I do. I can't hear the news. Please don't turn down the TV.
是的，這樣我會聽不到新聞。
請不要把電視的音量調小。

含「半邀請、半提議」的意思，而欲「徵求同意」的說法：

Shall I + 動詞？

Shall we + 動詞？

Shall I pick you up tonight?
我今天晚上去接你好嗎？

Shall we start the meeting?
我們開始開會好嗎？

Shall we go now?
我們現在出發嗎？

Shall we break for lunch now?
我們休息一下，吃個午餐好嗎？

凱特·史密斯（Kate Smith）請肯·史密斯（Khan Smith）把音樂的聲音調小一點……

潘·湯姆森（Pam Thomson）詢問柯提斯·凱博（Curtis Cabe）是否可以把冷氣關掉……

圖解6到66歲都學得會的**超簡單英語會話**

佩特察瑪・絲莉南（Phetchama Srinam）向彼得・史密斯（Peter Smith）請假……

May I take a few days off, please?

請問我可以請幾天假嗎？

Yes, you may. May I ask why?

好的，我可以問是為什麼嗎？

I have to attend my aunt's funeral.

我要去參加阿姨的葬禮。

It starts tomorrow in Yilan.

明天在宜蘭舉辦。

I'm sorry for your loss.

我感到很遺憾。

肯‧史密斯（Khan Smith）跟蘇珊‧沃登（Susan Wooden）提議
要去接她……

Shall I pick you up at 5 p.m.?
我下午 5 點去接妳好嗎？

Sure.
好。

威廉‧摩根（William Morgan）問佩特察瑪‧絲莉南（Phetchama
Srinam）他可不可以抽菸……

Would you mind
if I smoked here?
妳介意我在這裡抽菸嗎？

Yes, I would actually.
This is a non-smoking
area.
介意，這裡是禁菸區。

生活會話「**超簡單**」 20-06

丹·沃登（Dan Wooden）問凱特·史密斯（Kate Smith）他可不可以坐在她旁邊……

Note

Note

Chapter 21

第二十一章
你可以幫我開門嗎？
Making Requests & Asking for Help

請求他人或請求協助

如果我們有求於他人、打擾或請求他人的協助時，你會怎麼說？而這些句子又該如何用英文表達呢？這是我們這一章的學習重點，一起來看看吧！

你幫我……好嗎？

Can you + 動詞？

Could you + 動詞？

Would you + 動詞？

Will you + 動詞？

★ 「will」不是很有禮貌的說法。因此，「will」這個字彙，只能用在非常熟識的人之間，例如：家人、親戚和朋友。

Can you help me, please?
請問你可以幫我嗎?

Can you hold my handbag for a second?
你可以幫我拿一下包包嗎?

Could you help me with my homework?
你可以幫我寫作業嗎?

Could you give me some examples?
你可以舉一些例子嗎?

Would you do something for me, please?
請問你可以幫我做些事情嗎?

Would you please open the door for me?
請問你可以幫我開門嗎?

Will you come to my home tonight?
你今晚可以到我家嗎?

Will you buy me something to eat
on your way here?
你來這裡的路上,可以幫我買點吃的嗎?

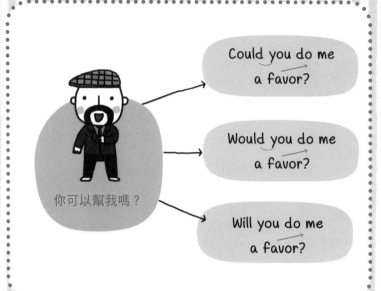

你可以幫我嗎？

Could you do me a favor?

Would you do me a favor?

Will you do me a favor?

「回應」要求、請求或協助

Yes.	好的。
Sure.	當然。
Certainly.	沒問題。
Of course.	當然。
O.K.	好的。
All right.	好。
With pleasure.	非常樂意。
I'd be glad to.	我很樂意。

「婉拒」要求、請求或協助

I'm sorry, but + 原因

I wish I could, but + 原因

I'm sorry,
but I'm using it tomorrow.
很抱歉，但是我明天要用。

I wish I could,
but I've lent it to Susan already.
我希望我幫得上忙，但我已經借給蘇珊了。

你介意⋯⋯嗎？

Would you mind + 動詞 ing?

Do you mind + 動詞 ing?

Would you mind lending me your car for two days?

你介意把車借給我兩天嗎？

Would you mind sending this file to Mr. Smith for me, please?

你介意幫我把這個檔案寄給史密斯先生嗎？

Do you mind lending me 2,000 dollars?

你介意借我 2000 塊嗎？

Do you mind typing all this information for me?

你介意幫我輸入這些資料嗎？

No, I don't.
I'd be glad to.

No, not at all.

No, certainly not.

不介意。
不介意幫忙。

Not at all.

Of course not.

Certainly not.

No, of course not.

丹‧沃登（Dan Wooden）請蘇珊‧沃登（Susan Wooden）幫他開燈⋯⋯

Can you turn on the lights, please?
妳可以把燈打開嗎？

O.K.
好的。

彼得‧史密斯（Peter Smith）請佩特察瑪‧絲莉南（Phetchama Srinam）幫她關門⋯⋯

Could you please shut the door?
請妳幫我關門好嗎？

Certainly.
好的。

柯提斯‧凱博（Curtis Cabe）請潘‧湯姆森（Pam Thomson）幫他找紙和筆……

Would you get me a pen and a piece of paper, please?

請問妳可以幫我找一支筆和一張紙嗎？

Of course, sir.

當然，先生。

Note

威廉‧摩根（William Morgan）請潘‧湯姆森（Pam Thomson）幫他影印……

Would you mind photocopying this document for me?
妳介意幫我印這份文件嗎？

No, not at all.
不，不介意。

Note

丹‧沃登（Dan Wooden）請肯‧史密斯（Khan Smith）借他
車……

Do you mind lending me your car
tomorrow?

你介意明天把車借給我嗎？

I wish I could, but I need it
tomorrow.

我希望可以，但我明天要用。

彼得‧史密斯（Peter Smith）請佩特察瑪‧絲莉南（Phetchama Srinam）幫他打電話，通知顧客他會晚一點到……

Could you do me a favor?
妳可以幫我一個忙嗎？

With pleasure.
非常樂意。

Please call Ms. Wooden and tell her I'll be late.
幫我打給沃登小姐說我會晚一點到。

Note

PART 3

Chapter 22

第二十二章
需要幫忙嗎？
Offering Assistance

提供協助的說法

上一個章節，我們學會「要求他人」或「請他人幫忙」的時候該如何表達。現在，我們要進一步學習「提供協助」時，該如何流暢地表達讓他人清楚瞭解，馬上一起來看看吧！

May I help you?

Can I help you with something?

Can I help you?

需要幫忙嗎？

Can I give you a hand?

Is there something I can help you with?

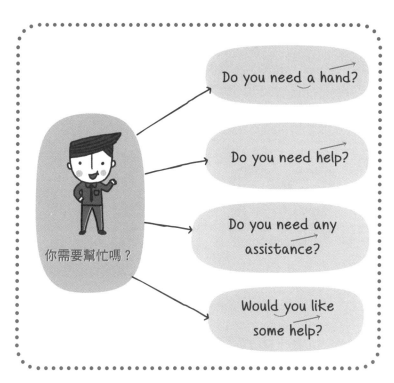

讓我⋯⋯。
Let me + 動詞

Let me help you.
讓我幫你。

Let me carry these books for you.
讓我幫你拿書。

Let me give you a ride.
讓我順道載你。

Let me give you a lift!
讓我載你吧！

Let me pick you up!
讓我去接你吧！

Let me buy you dinner!
讓我請你吃晚餐吧！

麗茲·沃登（Liz Wooden）到彼得·史密斯（PeterSmith）的公司洽公，在等待的時候，佩特察瑪·絲莉南（PhetchamaSrinam）過來詢問有沒有什麼需要……

Can I help you?
需要幫忙嗎？

Yes, please. Could you please tell me where the ladies' room is?
是的，請告訴我女廁在哪裡？

Yes. I'll show you.
Please come this way.
好的，我帶妳去，這邊請。

威廉‧摩根（William Morgan）看到彼得‧史密斯（Peter Smith）坐在公司裡很久了，因此詢問他是否需要幫忙……

Is there anything I can help you with?

有什麼我可以幫忙的嗎？

No, thank you. I'm waiting for Ms. Wooden. She's coming.

不，謝謝你。我正在等沃登小姐，她已經要過來了。

Note

Daily English Conversation

Note

Chapter 23

第二十三章
請問機場在哪裡？
Asking &
Giving Directions

關於「問路」的說法

如果你也是熱愛旅行的人，那麼「問路」這件事情，對你來說一定不陌生，應該更能深刻感覺到它的重要性。在這一個章節裡，我們除了要學習如何「問路」之外，同時也會介紹到，當他人向你「問路」的時候，你又該如何回應他人！

「Excuse me.」之後接上這些問題：

我要去……怎麼走？

請告訴我怎麼去……？

How do I get to...?

Could you please tell me how to get to...?

Could you please tell me where... is?

請告訴我怎麼去……

Excuse me. How do I get to the police station?

不好意思，請問警察局怎麼走？

Excuse me. Could you please tell me how to get to the post office?

不好意思，請問你可以告訴我郵局怎麼走嗎？

Excuse me. Could you please tell me where the nearest dentist is?

不好意思，請問你可以告訴我最近的牙醫診所在哪裡嗎？

「非正式」的「問路方式」

「Excuse me.」之後接上這些問句：

你知道……嗎？

……在哪裡嗎？

Do you know where... is?

Where is...?

I'm looking for...

I'm trying to find...

Excuse me.
Do you know
where the airport is?

不好意思，你知道機場在哪裡嗎？

Excuse me.
Where is the nearest public toilet?

不好意思，最近的公廁在哪裡呢？

……在哪裡？

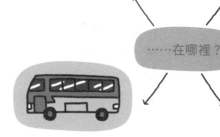

Excuse me.
Where is the bus station?

不好意思，公車站在哪裡呢？

Excuse me.
I'm trying to find a gas station.

不好意思，我正在找加油站。

Can you show it to me on the map?
你可以幫我在地圖上指出來嗎？

如果我們要詢問「**附近有什麼……嗎？**」，例如：「**這附近有醫院嗎？**」或「**這附近有百貨公司嗎？**」你可以這樣問：

附近有……嗎？

附近的……在哪裡？

Excuse me. Is there... near here?

Excuse me. Where is... around here?

Excuse me. Where is the nearest... around here?

附近有……嗎？

Excuse me.
Is there a beauty salon near here?

不好意思，附近有美容院嗎？

Excuse me.
Where is a laundry around here?

不好意思，附近有洗衣店嗎？

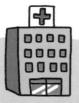

Excuse me.
Where is the nearest hospital around here?

不好意思，這裡最近的醫院在哪裡呢？

Daily English Conversation

「指引方向」或「指引地點」常用的說法

I'll show you.
我帶你去。

I'll show you on the map.
我在地圖上指出位置給你看。

Go along this street until you come to...
沿著這條路走，直到你走到……。

Keep walking until you see...
一直走到你看見……。

Keep driving until you see...
一直開到你看見……。

Then turn left into... Street.
接著左轉到……路。

Then turn right into... Street.
接著右轉到……路。

Go along this street until
you come to the T-junction.
Then turn left into Happy Street.

沿著這條路走到三叉路口，然後左轉至 Happy 路。

Keep walking until
you see the intersection.
Then turn left into ABC Street.

一直走到十字路口，然後左轉至 ABC 路。

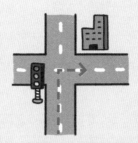

Keep walking until
you see the traffic lights.
Then turn right.

一直走到看見紅綠燈，然後右轉。

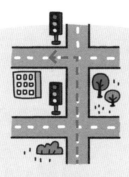

Keep driving until
you see the second set of traffic lights.
Then turn left.

一直開到你看見第二個紅綠燈，然後左轉。

When you get to..., turn into... Road.
當你到了……轉進……路。

When you come to..., turn left / right.
當你到了……，然後左轉／右轉。

When you get to the intersection, turn left.
當你到十字路口，左轉。

When you get to the junction, turn into Lucky Road.
當你到了路口，轉至 Lucky 路。

When you come to the third set of traffic lights, turn right.

當你到了第三個紅綠燈,右轉。

Drive past...　開過⋯⋯
Walk past...　走過⋯⋯

Drive past the police station.

開過警察局。

Walk past PPN University.

走過 PRN 大學。

It's on the left hand side.
它在左手邊。

It's on the right hand side.
它在右手邊。

It's on the corner of... Street.
它在……路的轉角。

It's next to...
它在……旁邊。

It's near...
它靠近……。

It's opposite...
它在……對面。

It's in front of...
它在……前面。

It's behind...
它在……後面。

It's on the corner
of Happy Street.

它在 Happy 路的轉角。

The hotel is on the left
hand side of Lucky Road.

那間旅館在 Lucky 路的左邊。

The market is opposite
to the hospital.

那個市場在醫院的對面。

「不知道怎麼走」時，你可以說……

I'm sorry. I don't know.
對不起，我不知道。

I'm sorry.
I have no idea.
對不起，我沒主意。

不知道該怎麼走時

I'm sorry.
I'm not from around here.
我不是這附近的人。

I'm afraid I can't help you.
我沒辦法告訴你。

麗茲・沃登（Liz Wooden）問佩特察瑪・絲莉南（Phetchama Srinam）廁所該往哪裡走……

Excuse me. Could you please tell me where the restroom is?

不好意思，請問廁所在哪裡？

Go down this corridor.
It's on the right hand side.

沿著這個走廊走，它在右手邊。

Thank you.

謝謝妳。

You're most welcome.

不客氣。

瑪萊‧史密斯（Malai Smith）不知道百貨公司的電器部門在哪裡，因此詢問陌生人……

Excuse me, could you please tell me where the electronics device section is?

不好意思，請問妳可以告訴我電器部門在哪裡嗎？

Sure. It's on the third floor, near the women's clothing section.

當然，它在三樓，靠近女裝部門。

Thank you.

謝謝妳。

You're welcome.

不客氣。

潘・湯姆森（Pam Thomson）在開車到醫院的路上，但是她迷路了。
她想知道離自己最近的醫院要怎麼走，所以她跟陌生人問路……

Excuse me, how do I get to the nearest hospital?

不好意思，最近的醫院該怎麼走呢？

Er... the nearest hospital from here is KNN Hospital.

呃……離這裡最近的醫院是 KNN 醫院。

Go along this street until you come to the intersection.

沿著這條路走到十字路口。

Cross the street.

然後過馬路。

I beg your pardon?
可以再說一次嗎？

When you come to the intersection, cross it.
當你開到十字路口，繼續開過去。

Keep driving until you see the shopping mall.
直到你看見購物中心。

The hospital is on the other side of the street, opposite the shopping mall.
那間醫院就在另一邊，購物中心的對面。

Thank you.
謝謝你。

My pleasure.
不客氣。

丹·沃登（Dan Wooden）正在過馬路，有人開車經過，並停下來問他路怎麼走……

Excuse me, could you tell me
how to get to the train station?

不好意思，你可以跟我說火車站要怎麼走嗎？

It's on Winyo Road,
next to Sukdee Market.

它在 Winyo 路上，靠近 Sukdee 市場。

Go along this street until you come
to the second set of traffic lights.

沿著這條路開到第二個紅綠燈。

Then turn left into Winyo Street.

然後左轉到 Winyo 路上。

The second set of traffic lights?
第二個紅綠燈嗎？

Yes, that's right.
是的。

Then turn left?
然後左轉？

Yes. Keep driving.
是的，繼續開。

Go past BKK Bank.
Then you'll see the market.
開過 BKK 銀行。
你就會看到市場了。

I'm sorry, go past what?
抱歉，開過什麼？

Go past BKK Bank.
Then you'll see Sukdee Market.
開過 BKK 銀行。
然後，你就會看到 Sukdee 市場。

The train station is between Sukdee Market and Sunny Hotel.
火車站在 Sukdee 市場跟 Sunny 旅館之間。

Daily English Conversation

第二十四章
我點的餐點還沒有來。
At a Restaurant

在餐廳裡的用語

　　「民以食為天」，你是否也喜歡喝下午茶？在高級餐廳用餐呢？在用餐的過程中，常會遇到那些狀況？這一個章節中，貼心地挑選出用餐時常用的英文用法及說法：從餐廳服務生的問句開始，介紹到如何點餐，準備好開始學習了嗎？

服務生詢問顧客

Good afternoon.
Welcome to Yummy Restaurant.
午安，歡迎蒞臨 Yummy 餐廳。

Good evening.
Happy Restaurant, welcome.
晚上好，Happy 餐廳，歡迎光臨。

Hello. Welcome to
Yenta Restaurant.
你好，歡迎光臨 Yenta 餐廳。

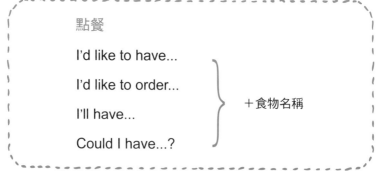

I'd like to have a salmon spicy salad.
我想要點辣鮭魚沙拉。

I'd like to order baked spareribs
with pineapple.
我想要點烤肋排佐鳳梨。

I'll have a sirloin beef steak.
我要點沙朗牛排。

Could I have a salmon steak?
我可以點鮭魚排嗎？

圖解6到66歲都學得會的**超簡單英語會話**

詢問「推薦菜單」時，你可以說：

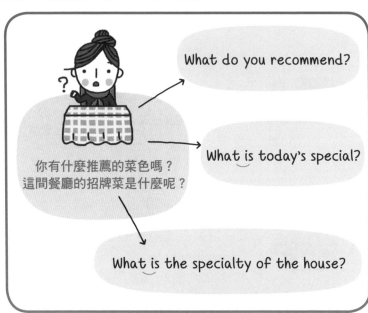

你有什麼推薦的菜色嗎？
這間餐廳的招牌菜是什麼呢？

What do you recommend?

What is today's special?

What is the specialty of the house?

我們的招牌菜
是……

Our recommended dishes are...

Today's special is...

May I recommend...?

I'll take it. 「決定點」這道菜 I'll have it.

Anything else? 還需要點些別的嗎？ Would you like to order anything else?

「覆誦」點菜清單

May I repeat your order? Let me repeat your order.

你有……嗎？

Do you have any...?

Have you got any...?

Do you have any salt?

你有鹽罐嗎？

Do you have any fish sauce?

你有魚露嗎？

詢問
「其他需求」

My order still hasn't arrived.

我點的餐點還沒來。

This is not what I ordered.

這不是我點的菜。

詢問
「點菜狀況」

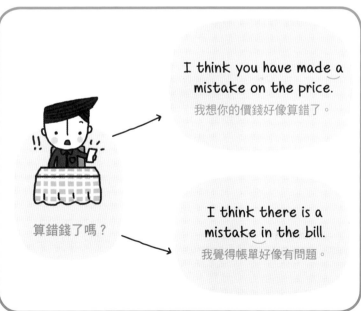

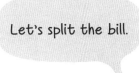

Let's split the bill.

Let's share the bill.

分開結帳。

Let me treat you next time.

下次我請你。

彼得・史密斯（Peter Smith）帶家人到餐廳來用餐……

How many people, sir?
先生，請問幾位呢？

Four people.
四位。

This way, please.
這邊請。

Please have a seat.
請坐。

May we have the menu?
可以給我們菜單嗎？

Certainly. Here you are.
當然，在這裡。

I'll be back in a few minutes to take your order.
我等一下再回來幫各位點餐。

3 分鐘後

Are you ready to order now?

準備要點餐了嗎？

Yes, we are.

是的。

I'll have a pork steak.

我要一份豬排。

How would you like your steak?

你的豬排要幾分熟呢？

Well done, please.

全熟。

I'd like a tuna salad.

我要一份鮪魚沙拉。

What do you recommend?
你有什麼推薦的嗎？

Our recommended dishes are salmon spicy salad, baked spareribs with pineapple,
我們的招牌菜是辣鮭魚沙拉、烤肋排佐鳳梨，

and spaghetti baby clams with chili paste cream sauce.
還有蛤蜊義大利麵佐辣奶油醬。

The spaghetti sounds delicious. I'll have that.
義大利麵聽起來很好吃。
我要點那個。

Me too.
我也是。

What would you like to drink?
要喝點什麼嗎？

We'll have two bottles of drinking water, a bottle of Coke
我們要兩罐水、一瓶可樂，

and a glass of orange juice.
還有一杯橘子汁。

May I repeat your order?
那我可以覆誦一次各位的餐點嗎？

A pork steak, a tuna salad, two dishes of spaghetti baby clams with chili paste cream sauce,
一份豬排、一份鮪魚沙拉、兩份蛤蜊義大利麵佐辣奶油醬、

two bottles of drinking water, a bottle of Coke and a glass of orange juice.
兩罐水、一瓶可樂還有一杯橘子汁。

Is that correct?
對嗎？

That's correct.
沒錯。

在用餐時……

O.K. Thank you, son.

好，謝謝你，兒子。

Thanks a lot, brother. Let me treat the three of you next time.

謝謝哥哥，下次換我請你們三個。

Sure. Or the two of us can split the bill next time if you want.

當然。如果你要的話，我們兩個下次可以一起分擔帳單。

All right.

好。

肯‧史密斯（Khan Smith）請服務生來結帳……

Waiter.
服務生。

Yes, sir.
是的，先生。

Check,
please.
請結帳。

One moment,
please.
請稍等一下。

服務生算錯錢了……

I think you have made a mistake
on the bill.
我想你帳單好像算錯了。

We ordered only one pork steak.
我們只有點一份豬排。

Oh, we're terribly sorry for our mistake.

噢，發生這個錯誤，我們深感抱歉。

That's all right.

沒關係。

Please wait for a few minutes. I'll give you the right change.

請稍等一下，我找正確的零錢給你。

蘇珊‧沃登（Susan Wooden）要點披薩，店員問她要內用還是外帶……

Good afternoon. Welcome to Yummy Pizza.
午安，歡迎光臨 Yummy 披薩。

What would you like to order?
妳要點些什麼呢？

I'd like a large size of bacon deluxe and six fried chicken wings.
我要一份大的豪華培根還有六支雞翅。

Eat in or to go?
內用還是外帶呢？

To go, please.
外帶。

The pizza will be ready in 15 minutes.
披薩再 15 分鐘就好了。

It's 320 altogether.
總共是 320 元。

Here you are.
這裡。

Thank you.
謝謝妳。

15 分鐘後

Your order is ready now.
Here you are.
妳的餐點已經好了，在這裡。

Thank you.
謝謝你。

You're welcome.
不客氣。

Please come again.
歡迎下次再來。

Chapter 25

第二十五章
這件外套可以算便宜一點嗎？
Shopping & Bargaining

和「購物」相關的用法

你也是瘋狂的購物者嗎？對喜歡血拚的人來說，「購物」和「議價」的用語絕對是非常重要的。在購物時，該如何跟店員殺價？店員跟你介紹產品或商品時，又會用到哪些句子呢？想要以低價購入各類商品，一定要好好學習這一個章節喔！

顧客回答自己需要什麼，回答「我在找……」

I'm looking for...

I'd like to buy...

Do you have any...?

May I see...?

May I have a look at...?

+ 正在找的東西

顧客詢問商品

Yes, please. I'm looking for a white skirt.
是的，我在找白色的裙子。

Yes, please. I'd like to buy two kilos of oranges.
是的，我想買兩公斤的橘子。

顧客詢問商品

Do you have any lettuce?
你們有萵苣嗎？

May I see that gold necklace please?
請讓我看看那條金項鍊好嗎？

No, thanks. I'm just looking.

No, thank you.

只是隨便逛逛。

Not right now, thank you.

May I try it on?
我可以試穿這件嗎？

May I try them on?
我可以試穿它們嗎？

Where is the fitting room?
試衣間在哪裡呢？

可以試穿嗎？

Does it fit you?

Do they fit you?

商品合適嗎？

有沒有別的尺寸呢？

Do you have it in size ...?
你們有這個款式的⋯⋯（尺寸）嗎？

Do you have it in a bigger size?
你們有大一點的尺寸嗎？

詢問尺寸

Do you have it in a smaller size?
你們有小一點的尺寸嗎？

Do you have it in 顏色？
這一款有⋯⋯色嗎？

圖解 6 到 66 歲都學得會的**超簡單英語會話**

詢問顏色

Do you have it in green?
你們這款有綠色的嗎?

詢問商品的問題

What size is it?
這是什麼尺寸呢?

What brand is it?
這是什麼牌子的呢?

What is it made of?
這是什麼製的?

Where was it made?
它的產地在哪裡?

詢問商品價錢

How much is it?

How much does it cost?

詢問商品價錢

How much is this watch?
這支錶多少錢呢？

How much is a bottle of fish sauce?
這罐魚露多少錢？

How much does a kilo of oranges cost?
一公斤橘子要多少錢？

詢問多件商品的價錢

How much are they?

How much do they cost?

詢問多件商品的價錢

How much are these 2 watches?

這兩支錶多少錢呢？

How much are 2 bottles of fish sauce?

這兩罐魚露多少錢？

How much do two kilos of oranges cost?

兩公斤橘子要多少錢？

如果我們購買很多件不一樣的東西，要請店員計算全部的金額，可以這麼說：

提出自己期望的價格

How about 100 dollars?
可以算 100 元嗎？

I can give you... % discount.
I can let you have it for...

可以有多少
折扣呢？

I can give you a
10% discount.
我可以幫你打 9 折。

I can let you have it
for 450 dollars.
我可以算你 450 元就好。

還需要
別的東西嗎？

Anything else?

Would you like to
buy anything else?

Is there anything
else you need?

Yes, please.
是的。

No, that's all.
不用，這樣就好了。

顧客

顧客

潘・湯姆森（Pam Thomson）跟佩特察瑪・絲莉南（Phetchama Srinam）去購物……

Good afternoon.
May I help you?
午安，需要什麼服務嗎？

Yes. Can I see the blue blouse
on the shelf, please?
是的，我可以看一下櫥窗裡那件藍色罩衫嗎？

Of course. Here you go.
當然，在這裡。

This is the newest pattern.
這是最新的款式。

Do you have it in white?
有白色的嗎？

圖解6到66歲都學得會的**超簡單英語會話**

Yes, we do. What size would you like?
有的，妳想要什麼尺寸呢？

Medium, please.
M 的，麻煩。

Just a moment, please. Here you are.
請稍等一下，在這裡。

May I try it on?
我可以試穿嗎？

Yes, you may. The fitting room is over there.
可以，試衣間在那邊。

在潘去試穿的時候……

Can I help you with something?
有什麼需要服務的嗎？

Do you have this pair of sneakers in a bigger size?
你們這雙休閒鞋有大一點的尺寸嗎？

These ones are too small for me.
這雙對我來說太小了。

I'm sorry. These are the last pair left in this color.
抱歉，這是這個顏色的最後一雙了。

We have black, brown and white ones in size 34.
34 號的我們還有黑色、咖啡色和白色。

May I see the brown ones, please?
可以讓我看一下咖啡色的嗎？

Wait a minute, please. Here you are.
請稍等一下,在這裡。

 Would you like to try them on?
妳想要試穿看看嗎?

 Yes, please.
好的。

 Do they fit your feet?
有合妳的腳嗎?

Yes, they do. How much do they cost?
有,這雙多少錢呢?

 They're on sale for 750 dollars.
現在特價 750 元。

O.K. I'll take them.
好，我買了。

Here you are.
錢在這裡。

Let me put them in a bag for you.
我幫妳裝袋。

3 分鐘後

Here are your sneakers and here is your change.
Thank you.
這裡是妳的休閒鞋和零錢，謝謝妳。

潘‧湯姆森（Pam Thomson）試穿衣服後，詢問店員是否可以打折……

How about 400 dollars?

可以算 400 元嗎？

No, I'm sorry.

不行，很抱歉。

OK. I'll take it.

好，我買了。

Here you are, 500 dollars.

這裡，500 元。

Thank you.
Here's 50 dollars change.

謝謝妳，這是零錢 50 元。

瑪萊‧史密斯（Malai Smith）和凱特‧史密斯（Kate Smith）到手錶店……

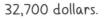
32,700 dollars.
32,700 元。

It's beautiful, isn't it?
它很漂亮，不是嗎？

Yes, it is. But it isn't my style.
是的，但它不是我想要的款式。

Let me look around for a while, please!
讓我先到處看看吧！

Of course, ma'am.
Let me know when you need anything.
沒問題，太太。有什麼需要，請讓我知道。

瑪萊正在挑選手錶……

Would you like some help?
妳需要什麼服務嗎？

No, thanks.
I'm just looking.
不，謝謝，我只是隨便看看。

May I have a look at that watch, please?
我可以看看那支手錶嗎？

Here it is.
在這裡。

What is it made of?
這是用什麼做的？

It's made of silver.
這是銀製的。

What brand is it?

是什麼牌子的？

GK.

GK。

Where was it made?

它是哪裡生產的？

It was made in Switzerland.

是瑞士生產的。

How much is it?

多少錢呢？

6,400 dollars.

6,400 元。

Can you reduce the price?

可以算便宜一點嗎？

I'm sorry, this is a reasonable price.

很抱歉，這個價位算很合理了。

凱特・史密斯（Kate Smith）在市場買肉和雞蛋……

Can I help you?
需要什麼服務嗎？

Yes, please.
是的。

I'd like to buy 300 grams of pork, 200 grams of beef, and 12 chicken wings, please.
我要買 300 克的豬肉、200 克的牛肉和 12 支雞翅。

Anything else?
還要什麼嗎？

Yes. Do you sell eggs?
是的，你有賣雞蛋嗎？

Yes, we do. How many do you want?
有的，妳需要幾顆呢？

How do you sell them?
雞蛋怎麼賣？

40 dollars per dozen.
一打 40 元。

I'd like to buy a dozen eggs, please.

我要一打雞蛋，麻煩了。

That's all. How much is that altogether?

就這樣，總共多少錢呢？

That'll be 360 dollars.

總共 360 元。

Here you are.

這裡。

Here's 40 dollars change.

這裡是零錢 40 元。

Thank you.

謝謝你。

Chapter 26

第二十六章
你有對任何藥物過敏嗎？
Illness

醫生與病人對話時的用語

　　最後一個主題，應該不會有人想要碰到，但它卻是生活中很難避免的。每個人難免會遇到有病痛的時候。因此，這一章我們要學的就是如何跟醫生闡述自己的病症及瞭解醫生通常都會問哪些問題。

How long have you been sick?
你不舒服多久了？

Have you taken any medications?
你有吃其他的藥品嗎？

醫生會問的問題

Let me examine you.
讓我檢查看看。

Have you put anything on it?
你有敷什麼其他的藥嗎？

Do you have a fever?
你有發燒嗎？

Are you allergic to any medications?
你有對任何藥物過敏嗎？

各種病狀的說法

I have a headache.

我頭痛。

I have a fever.

我發燒了。

I have a cold.

我感冒了。

I feel dizzy.

我頭暈。

I've been coughing.

我一直咳嗽。

I've got a sore throat.

我喉嚨痛。

I have a runny nose.

我流鼻涕。

I have a stomachache.

我胃痛。

I have an earache.

我耳朵痛。

I have a sore eye.

我眼睛痛。

I have a toothache.

我牙痛。

I've got a backache.

我背部痛。

I've got pain in my chest.

我胸口痛。

I've got diarrhoea.

我拉肚子了。

I've been throwing up.

我嘔吐了。

I'm allergic to seafood.

我對海鮮過敏。

蘇珊・沃登（Susan Wooden）感冒了，所以去看醫生……

Good morning. Please take a seat.
早安，請坐。

What seems to be the problem?
妳怎麼了嗎？

I feel dizzy. I have a runny nose and a sore throat.
我覺得頭暈，流鼻涕還有喉嚨痛。

I've been coughing.
我一直咳嗽。

Let me examine you.

讓我檢查一下。

Please take deep breaths in and out. Well done.

請深呼吸，吸氣再吐氣，很好。

Can I take your blood pressure?

我可以量一下妳的血壓嗎？

Let me feel your pulse.

我量一下脈搏。

Can I take your temperature?

我可以量一下妳的體溫嗎？

Open your mouth wide. Very good.

張開嘴巴，很好。

Are you allergic to any medications?
妳有對任何藥物過敏嗎？

No, I'm not.
沒有。

I'll give you a prescription.
我會給妳處方籤。

Take 2 tablets 3 times a day after meals.
三餐飯後，吃 2 顆藥丸。

You need to rest a lot more. Drink plenty of water.
妳要多休息、多喝水。

Keep warm and get some exercise.
保持溫暖，然後運動。

If you don't feel better within a week, please come back to see me.

如果一個禮拜後還是沒有好轉，請再回來讓我檢查。

Can I have a medical certificate, please?

請問我可以拿就醫證明嗎？

Certainly. You should take sick leave for 2 days.

當然，妳應該請 2 天病假。

Thank you, doctor.

謝謝你，醫生。

You're welcome.

不客氣。

新多益考試有祕密

30天挑戰新多益600分

準備新多益，就從「考題」下手

《新多益考試有祕密：30天挑戰新多益600分》
2書＋1MP3（附防水書套） 定價／**379**元

獨家附贈

新多益全球化祕密
單字隨身書

30天學習計劃，馬上破解「新多益考試的祕密」！

30天 學習計劃，熟悉新多益考試題目─800道題目，完整破解新多益考試7大題型！
30天 學習計劃，累積新多益考試重點─800道題目，單字、片語、文法重點學習！
30天 學習計劃，破解新多益考試祕密─800道題目，反覆練習加強應考實力！

利用「短句」＋「短句」的方式，
說一口漂亮的英文！！！

英文要說得漂亮，
就該簡短有力！！

與老外交談，除了 How are you?
和 Sorry, I don't know. 之外，
你還會哪些英文短句呢？

一應俱全的
英文口語練習書
- 最全面的主題！
- 最關鍵的單字！
- 最實用的短句！

四大場合完全適用
- 求職面試 ● 商務出差
- 出國旅遊 ● 短期留學

1書＋1MP3
定價／**299元**

★ 只要你敢開口，保證連老外都會讚嘆！

我識出版集團　　我識客服：(02) 2345-7222　http://www.17buy.com.tw
　　　　　　　　我識傳真：(02) 2345-5758　jam.group@17buy.com.tw
〔全國各大書店熱烈搶購中！大量訂購，另有折扣〕
劃撥帳號：19793190　戶名：我識出版社

國中三年、高中三年、大學四年，
學了10年的英文，
你用的英文都正確嗎？

我讀英文 091

95% 會用錯的英文

要用就要用得正確！

戴媺凌 編著

95% 會用錯的英文

學了就要用，要用就要用得正確！！

國中三年、高中三年、大學四年，學了10年的英文，你用的英文都正確嗎？找回那些曾學過、且真正用得上的英文，讓10年所學英語不白費！

單字選對了，英文就準了！
片語說對了，老外都讚嘆！
文法用對了，思維就對了！

★ FREE ★
獨家附贈
學習筆記＋重點
提示彩色標籤
貼紙

學了10年英文，為什麼還是會用錯單字？
contract和treaty都有「合約、規約」的解釋，為什麼不可以互換使用？如果只是硬梆梆地背7,000、7,000甚至20,000的英文單字，所全被解單字的真正涵義，這樣為文章字彙會有問題的！

學了10年英文，為什麼還是會用錯片語？
die from和die of同樣都有「死亡」的意思，介系詞雖然，死前就太不同，如果只是死背會話片語不懂靈活運用，這樣英文片語還是用得不適恰！

學了10年英文，為什麼還是會用錯文法？
假設語氣的動詞該用過去式還是完成式？用錯時態不懂，無法正確傳達意思。如果只是牢記文法慣例或例句，這樣還是永遠英文內的生成毋庸，像老外一樣用得很自然！

➔ **絕對適合！**
● 剛開始學英文的你，建立正確的英文基礎。
● 就讀英文科系的你，破解老師不教的英文。
● 工作一段時間的你，改掉常犯的英文錯誤。

《95%會用錯的英文》
全書內容選自
〔升大學必考7,000單字〕
〔狄克森片語〕
〔九年一貫必備文法〕

I'm 我讀

● contract和treaty都有「合約、條約」的意思，為什麼不可以互換使用？

● die from和die of同樣都有「死亡」的意思，「死於癌症」該用哪個表示？

● 假設語氣的動詞該用過去式還是完成式？

《95%會用錯的英文》
幫你找回那些曾學過、
且真正用得上的英文，
讓10年所學英語不白費

★ FREE ★
獨家附贈
學習筆記＋重點
提示彩色標籤
貼紙

定價／299元

— 全書內容選自 —

升大學必考7,000單字
狄克森片語
九年一貫必備文法
學英文必備！！！

絕對適合：
☑ 剛開始學英文的你，建立正確的英文基礎。
☑ 就讀英文科系的你，破解老師不教的英文。
☑ 工作一段時間的你，改掉常犯的英文錯誤。

I'm 我識出版集團

我識客服：(02) 2345-7222　http://www.17buy.com.tw
我識傳真：(02) 2345-5758　iam.group@17buy.com.tw

〔全國各大書店熱烈搶購中！大量訂購，另有折
劃撥帳號▲19793190 戶名▲我識出版社

國家圖書館出版品預行編目（CIP）資料

圖解6到60歲都學得會的超簡單英語會話
（Daily English Conversation）／Thipthida
Butchui 著. 梁震牧 譯. -- 初版. -- 臺北市：
我識, 2014. 03 面；公分

ISBN 978-986-5785-20-8（平裝附光碟片）

1. 英語 2. 會話

805.188   103000593

圖解Graphic
6到60歲都學得會的
超簡單
英語會話

書名 / 圖解6到60歲都學得會的超簡單英語會話
作者 / Thipthida Butchui
譯者 / 梁震牧
發行人 / 蔣敬祖
編輯顧問 / 常祈天
主編 / 戴媺凌
執行編輯 / 謝昀蓁・曾羽辰
視覺指導 / 黃馨儀
內文排版 / 健呈電腦排版股份有限公司
法律顧問 / 北辰著作權事務所蕭雄淋律師
印製 / 金濱印刷事業有限公司
初版 / 2014年03月
出版 / 我識出版集團－我識出版社有限公司
電話 / (02) 2345-7222
傳真 / (02) 2345-5758
地址 / 台北市忠孝東路五段372巷27弄78之1號1樓
郵政劃撥 / 19793190
戶名 / 我識出版社
網址 / www.17buy.com.tw
E-mail / iam.group@17buy.com.tw
facebook網址 / www.facebook.com/ImPublishing
定價 / 新台幣 349 元 / 港幣 116 元（附1MP3）
Daily English Conversation © 2012, Proud Publisher. All rights reserved.
Traditional Chinese language translation rights arranged with I'm Publishing
Group Ltd., through Little Rainbow Agency.

台灣地區總經銷 / 采舍國際有限公司
地址 / 新北市中和區中山路二段366巷10號3樓

港澳總經銷 / 和平圖書有限公司
地址 / 香港柴灣嘉業街12號百樂門大廈17樓
電話 / (852) 2804-6687 傳真 / (852) 2804-6409